Don't Fu#k with My Heart

Lock Down Publications
Presents
Don't Fu#k with My Heart
A Novel by Linnea

Stay Connected with Us!

Text **LOCKDOWN** to 22828 to stay up-to-date with new releases, sneak peaks, contests and more…
Or CLICK HERE to sign up.

Thank you!

Like our page on Facebook:

Lock Down Publications: Facebook

Join Lock Down Publications/The New Era Reading Group

Follow us on Instagram:

Lock Down Publications: Instagram

Email Us**:** We want to hear from you!

Submission Guideline.

Submit the first three chapters of your completed manuscript to ldpsubmissions@gmail.com, subject line: Your book's title. The manuscript must be in a .doc file and sent as an attachment. Document should be in Times New Roman, double spaced and in size 12 font. Also, provide your synopsis and full contact information. If sending multiple submissions, they must each be in a separate email.

Have a story but no way to send it electronically? You can still submit to LDP/Ca$h Presents. Send in the first three chapters, written or typed, of your completed manuscript to:

LDP: Submissions Dept
Po Box 870494
Mesquite, Tx 75187

DO NOT send original manuscript. Must be a duplicate.

Provide your synopsis and a cover letter containing your full contact information.

Thanks for considering LDP and Ca$h Presents.

Don't Fu#k With My Heart

Visit our website www.lockdownpublications.com

Copyright 2014 by Linnea Don't Fu#k with My Heart

Lock Down Publications
Email: Authoresslinnea@gmail.com
Facebook: Authoress Linnea Ldp
Cover design and layout by: Dynasty's Cover Me
Book interior design by: Shawn Walker
Edited by: Epic Kreationz

Before I get started I have to give my "shout outs" to those that are important to me.

To my son, Kieran. I love you more than life itself. You have been my motivation to continue when I have wanted so desperately to give up. You've shown me the true meaning of unconditional love.

To my Momma, Daddy and Joe. You have been there in everything I do whether it has been a success or a failure. The word "no" was hardly ever in y'all vocabulary and if it was it had the best intentions. Words can describe my love and gratitude for y'all.

To my sister, Glynn. I pray this shows you that any dream is attainable with faith and hard work. Nothing will ever come easy. One day you'll become a fabulous makeup artist to the stars.

My cousin, Ranesha, keep pushing cuz. I love you and my girls.

To Myosha, my only ride or die since elementary. My classmate that I used to kick in the legs under our desks. I never fathomed in the 4th grade that we would be friends all these years later. The best is yet to come.

Alicia, Yondell, Kyande and Ashley. I'm so thankful I came home to find you ladies after Katrina. Y'all have kept me grounded so many days, helping to transform into the person I am today. It definitely hasn't been an easy road, but I'm almost there.

My two rays of sunshine, Lakiesha and Caz. It's a great thing that I don't believe in the saying "No New Friends" because I would have never been blessed with the gift of your friendship. My god babies have added so much joy to me and Kieran's life.

Ellen, Defreda, Bjorn, Emika, and Antoneka. Thanks girls for being a part of my huge support network.

Erica, I'm ecstatic you got me back into reading which opened the blessing of being able to meet such great literary authors.

NeNe Capri, my big sister who showed me how humble great writers can be. You took me in as a friend with no skepticism or questions asked. I'll always have mad love for you, Diva.

My mentor Ca$h. You have definitely been rough, but I believe it is all in love. When I sat down to type, I never imagined that I would be here thousands of words later. For the idea to write and the encouragement on days when I wanted to throw in the towel on this book, I salute you, Chief. You are a great friend and you make the Lock Down family proud of your everyday accomplishments despite the circumstances.

To the remainder of my Lock Down family: Coffee, Tranay Adams, Frank Gresham, Forever Redd, Royal Nicole, Ms. Writer for Life, Sandy Barrett Sims, Shawn Walker, Lady Stiletto, Latisha Lewinson and J Peach. You are the absolute best. This is more than a publishing company, but an extended part of my family. Let's continue to build this empire together.

My fans and supporters that took time to purchase my work. I can't be successful without you.

Finally, I dedicate this book to Ray. Some called you "Big Sho" but I called you my brother. It's still hard to believe that you are gone after almost twenty years of friendship. I don't know that there will ever be a more genuine person I will cross on this earth. I miss you each and every day. Love you always.

To anyone else I forgot, charge it to my head and not my heart. I'll catch you in the next.

Don't Fu#k With My Heart

Chapter 1

I sat on the defendant's side of family court, anxiously waiting for the judge to come out of his chamber and render the verdict. His ruling would either bring me joy or turn my whole world upside down, depending on which way the decision went.

Oh, my God! I thought as my hands began to shake and my palms grew sweaty. I could barely hold the ink pen steady as I scribbled nervously on the notepad that sat in front of me on the table. After a moment of jotting down my fears, I glanced down at what I had scrawled.

Please, Lord, don't let them take my baby away from me. Amen.

My prayer flashed up at me in large letters that took up the entire page. I inhaled deeply in a last attempt to calm myself, but my heart continued to pound rapidly in my chest.

Peering intensely at the wall clock, I focused my attention there as the minutes ticked by at a snail's pace. Out of the corner of my eye I saw my lowdown ass baby daddy, Quameer, sitting next to his bitch, Mariah. As much as I hated him for what he was doing to me, my contempt for his ho was even worse. Mariah wasn't just some random chick, she was my fucking step-sister! The way he'd waltzed into the courtroom with that white bitch by his side had my blood boiling. *These ratchet assholes,* I thought to myself as I stared daggers at the both of them.

Mariah was a black girl in white skin. She had long, blonde hair that flowed midway down her back and ocean blue eyes that had obviously mesmerized Quameer. But that's where the Caucasian ended and the Black began. She had a body like a sistah and the homegirl-type swag to match. All the guys were crazy about her, so I guess it made

Quameer feel privileged or something to have cuffed the white tramp. I had known years ago when my mother married her father that the bitch would be nothing but trouble. She resented the bond me and her father, Craig, shared. He was more like my blood father than the man I inherited through my mother's union with him, and Mariah was jealous of that. To say that I hated that *thot* would be an understatement.

I cut my eyes away from Mariah and pierced Quameer with a hard gaze. The arrogant look on his face was one that I knew well and it took me to a place where I couldn't help but remember what had attracted me to his sorry ass in the first place. He was five feet, ten inches tall with a dark brown, coffee complexion, and he had the sexiest brown bedroom eyes I'd ever looked into. He definitely had a charm about himself that would blow a woman's mind. Too bad he'd turned out to be my worst fucking nightmare.

I gnashed my teeth together as the pain and anger of Quameer's betrayal surged through my body and sent homicidal thoughts racing through my mind. *Calm down, Krissett,* I warned myself. *If you act a fool that'll only give the judge cause to rule in his favor.*

I unclenched my teeth and slowly counted to ten. When my breathing returned to normal, I looked over to the other side of the courtroom at my supporters. My momma and my grandmother, Hattie Mae, were there along with my brother, Quincy, and my best friend since fifth grade, Meishelle. And so was Stone, my new boyfriend. Not only were they were all in attendance, they were seated in the front of courtroom so the judge would know I had family and friends who believed in me.

Stone flashed me a reassuring smile that did little to make me feel better. "Don't worry, baby, everything will work out fine," he mouthed.

I forced a smile on my face and tried to soak up some of Stone's confidence, but trepidation snuffed it out. Just as I felt a panic attack coming on, I heard the bailiff's voice boom, "All rise for the Honorable Judge Washington." As I stood to my feet, I silently beseeched the Lord to be merciful to me and allow the decision to be in my favor.

Judge Washington, a tall, stately, black man, who appeared to be in his late fifties sat down at the bench high above us as if he was God himself. "You may be seated," he instructed the courtroom.

His expression gave no indication as to which way he would rule, but thank God, with no hesitation he began. "After review of the evidence presented, and having taken into account the numerous suicide attempts by the mother, it is the court's ruling that temporary custody of the minor, Na'Siah Johnson, be awarded to his father, Quameer Johnson."

"Noooooo!" I jumped out of my seat and slammed my palms down on the table, sending pen and paper flying to the floor. My hands stung from the fierce impact as I lifted them to my face and covered my eyes. "*Please*, Your Honor, don't take my baby away from me! You can't. *Please!*" I sobbed uncontrollably.

"Counselor, please advise Ms. Baptiste to have a seat and remain quiet or I will have to hold her in contempt of court," he sternly directed my attorney.

Mr. Daniels looked over at me and whispered, "Krissett, you've got to get ahold of yourself. The judge won't tolerate these outbursts. Please, try to remain calm."

Through my tears I saw his mouth continue to move, but I couldn't make out the rest of his warning. All I could think about were the nine months I had carried Na'Siah inside of me and the eight hours, twenty-three minutes, and twelve seconds of excruciating, painful labor I had endured to bring him into this world. And in the snap of a finger this mutha-fucka thought that he was going to take my child away from me, like that black robe he was wearing gave him power to overrule *my* God given right of motherhood.

I stood lost in a daze as the oxygen threatened to leave my lungs. I tried as hard as I could to gain control, but I couldn't. My chest heaved violently in and out as I gasped to catch my breath. The more I stood contemplating what the judge said, the more I could feel my world shattering into tiny pieces. My heart ached as if a wooden stake had been driven directly through the middle of it and pierced my soul. It was at that moment that my mind went blank and I lost it.

I lowered my hands to my sides and clenched my fists so hard that my nails dug into my skin. "Your Honor, you don't have the right to take my baby from me!" I screamed in a high pitch. "*God* gave me custody when He allowed me to conceive!"

Boom! Boom! Boom! The gavel slapped the bench and the sound echoed off of the courtroom walls. "Ms. Baptiste, you are out of order," he firmly raised his voice.

"I'm sorry," I sobbed as my body trembled violently. "My baby is all I have. *Please*!" I cried out. "I'm begging you, don't take him away from me. *I'm his mother*!" I fell to my knees in a prayer-like position. My tears flowed non-stop. "Please, Your Honor, I know I've made mistakes in my life, but I love my son. I would give my life for him." I continued pleading, pouring my heart out. The pain I felt was like nothing I had ever experienced before.

Mr. Daniels reached down and helped me back to my feet. I slowly stood and looked directly in the judge's eyes, praying, hoping, and wishing, my own eyes would tell the story of a mother's love.

When the judge looked at me and shook his head in dismay, I knew my plea had fallen on deaf ears.

My attorney gave me a moment to gather what little strength I had left before guiding me back to my seat. "Krissett, please don't make this any worse than it already is. You have to allow him to finish," he admonished in a low, but firm tone.

I wanted to spit in his face, but my mouth was as dry as cotton. Tears continued to flood my cheeks and my legs could no longer support me. I collapsed down in the chair and lowered my head on the table as my sobs became louder and my body rocked from the instant heartache.

Speaking above the sound of my pain, the judge continued on dispassionately. "Ms. Baptiste, based on your erratic behavior, which is well-documented in these reports, I have no other choice but to do this. The court will grant temporary custody of the minor to Mr. Johnson. You will be allowed unsupervised visitation with the minor each weekend at the times set by the court. I will revisit the conditions of this case at a later date."

I lifted my head and glowered at him with fire shooting from my eyes. "Why would you do this to me?" I roared.

"Ms. Baptiste, I suggest you get yourself together before the next hearing on this matter," he replied coldly.

As hard as I tried to remain calm and contain the outburst that I could feel bubbling up in my chest, I just couldn't do it. When I looked over at Quameer and Mariah wearing the look of victory on their faces, I felt as though they were silently taunting me.

Quameer winked at me and smirked.

That's when I lost it.

Before I knew what was happening, my inner demon had taken total control and everything I was thinking started to pour out. My hatred toward him and his cutthroat slut filled the courtroom.

I spun around to face that nigga and spat, "You *mutha-fucka*! How *could* you? You come in this courtroom pretending to be a loving father, but you stand there with her, who you fucked behind my back. Why don't you tell the judge about that, Quameer?" The pain in my heart caused my voice to rise two octaves.

"Ms. Baptiste!" The judge shouted. "Order in the court!" He banged the gavel down on the bench with so much fury that it went flying out of his hand and struck the court reporter upside the head.

"Ahhh!" She cried out.

Judge Washington shot up to his feet. "Mr. Daniels, calm your client or I will have her thrown in jail," the thunder in his threat reverberated loudly.

My attorney threw his arms up in exasperation. He knew that I could not be quieted. Hell to the fuck no. I was seething and beyond caring about the consequences.

I pointed my finger at my no-good baby daddy and jabbed the air like I was poking his chest with a knife. "Nigga, you may have fooled the court, but you and I both know you're nothin' but a punk-ass, dead beat father. You don't give a shit about our son. You're just doing this to hurt me. I hate you!" I venomously spewed.

Quameer opened his punk ass mouth to say something, but Mariah tugged on his sleeve, distracting him from his rant. She leaned in to whisper in his ear, but I read her dick sucking lips.

14

"Don't let that crazy heifer play you out of pocket, baby," she snootily said. Then she turned her nose up at me like she was all of that.

My hair almost burst into flames. "Bitch, you're nothing but a two-dollar tramp," I yelled. "You may enjoy my lefto-vers, but you'll never play mother to my son. Not fuckin' *ever!*"

"Order, there will be order in this courtroom immedi-ately," the judge shouted as he brought both palms down on the wooden desk repeatedly.

I looked up at him and saw that his yellow complexion had turned two shades of red. The courtroom filled with whispers and gasps from the onlookers, and my attorney stood looking at me with widened eyes of disappointment.

"Ms. Baptiste, you have been warned. I will not tolerate profanity in my courtroom. If you continue with these out-bursts you will be detained for contempt of court. For the final time, do I make myself clear?" Judge Washington barked at me.

I slowly shook my head *yes*. Tears flooded my face as I looked to my attorney to protect me from the judge's wrath. That's when Quameer's attorney shot to his feet.

"Your Honor," he began in a calm tone. He fastened his suit jacket, stepped from behind the table, and continued. "My client feels strongly that any contact between the minor and the defendant at this time would be harmful. We petition the court to add the stipulation that any visitation between Ms. Baptiste and the minor be supervised."

I was furious.

I sprang back to my feet and strongly protested. "I don't need any damn body to watch me with my son. Na'Siah was all I had when this sperm donating m'fer left us."

"*Ms. Baptiste!*" The judge shouted. "Young lady, your actions here today have not been positive. And that's putting it mildly." His eyes bore into mine and he continued on in a harsh, reprimanding tone. "I've been as lenient as I can be. I've given you a pass today only because you are the child's mother and I understand your emotion. However, I should've held you in contempt at your first outburst," he made mention.

"We apologize, Your Honor," my attorney cut in. He placed his arms around my shoulders and guided me down into my seat. "Krissett, please," he muttered. "These outbursts will only make the judge more likely to side with Mr. Johnson, permanently."

"This is my son we are talking about. They keep referring to him as the *minor* as if he's just some random-ass person. My blood runs through his body just as much as Mr. Johnson's over there does," I whispered tersely.

"Okay, but you have to keep calm and let me do what I've been retained to do."

"Well, you better do something fast," I snarled.

Mr. Daniels stood back up to make his argument. "Your Honor, the request Mr. Johnson and his attorney have suggested is absolutely ridiculous. There is no documented abuse of the minor by my client that would substantiate such a need."

Nodding his head, the Judge looked over to Quameer. "Mr. Williams, the court will not consider any other petitions at this time. The judgment will stand as ordered. Court is adjourned," he said with a single bang of the gavel, indicating the finality of his decree.

The world began to move in slow motion as I sat paralyzed by the weight of the decision. Powerless to change the injustice that I felt I'd been served, I cried hysterically as

Judge Washington got up from the bench and disappeared into his chamber. My attorney went over to talk to my family, as I remained seated, staring up at the vacant bench.

This can't be real, I thought. I had been taking all of my medication, trying so hard to get back on track for my baby. Quameer had abandoned us well over a year ago. I was the one who called my momma to come and get Na'Siah, realizing that I wasn't able to care for him in my depressed state. I loved my son. Quameer didn't even call once to see if Na'Siah needed formula, pampers, whatever. Then his butt pops back up and gets temporary custody. *How was that fair?* I asked the Heavens.

My mother and Quincy came around the seating area and rushed over to me. Quincy and I had always been very close growing up. We were like two peas in a pod, and no matter what I'd gone through in life, I could always remember him being there for me. This time was no different.

He kneeled down in front of my chair, gently placed his hands on the sides of my face and wiped my tears with his thumbs. "I know you're hurting, sis, but this is only temporary." He paused, choosing his words carefully, "The attorney says if you can demonstrate to the court that you're mentally stable and can provide for Na'Siah, he's positive that you'll get him back."

"Yeah, baby," my momma chimed in, hugging me from behind. "You know with every trial comes a victory. In life, only the strong survive. You have to learn not to give up and not to feel the need to give in so quickly," she reassured me with her words of wisdom. "No battle is ever truly lost until we stop fighting. I know this is a hard pill to swallow, but you have to dig deep and find your courage, your strength, your will," she paused before finishing. "More than any-thing, baby girl, you gotta fight this thing with love. A mother's love."

At that very moment I understood exactly what my mother was trying to say to me. I understood that if the love I had for my son was as strong and unconditional as I'd said it was, nothing and no one could stop me from getting him back. I let my tears continue to flow freely, unashamed to let my pain show.

"You stay focused on the prize, which is getting your baby back home where he belongs, and through faith and change you will come out the victor," my mother said as she tilted my head up toward hers so our eyes could make direct contact.

Still seated, I turned around to face my grandmother, Hattie Mae. She was the glue that held my family together. It was because of her that I wasn't in even worse shape after having hit rock bottom. No matter how bad things got, Hattie Mae never let me give up.

"What about the party we'd already planned for his third birthday?" I asked Hattie Mae, allowing my mind to wander aimlessly as I remained in a daze.

"It's on a weekend, remember, baby? We can still have it," she reassured me with a smile. "We'll all have a great time, too," she added.

"Why does God hate me so much?" I asked, as I restarted the waterworks. With all I had been through at such a young age, I couldn't see any other reason why He would allow something like that to happen to me.

"God does no such thing. He's given you back to me a million times when you'd taken it upon yourself to try and leave this earth. He will give you Na'Siah back when the time is right," she said, trying to give me back the hope I'd lost.

I nodded my understanding, but I had little faith. Never in a million years did I envision my life going in such a bad direction. But ever since I was diagnosed with mania, a condition that elevates the senses, often comparable to bipolar disorder, my days had been filled with depression. For the most part I was getting better daily, but just as fate would have it, something always came back to fuck with my sanity. The episode I'd just had was one of them.

Stone's deep voice penetrated through the cloud of my gloom. "Come on, Krissett. We have to leave now," he insisted. "That nigga won today, but it ain't over, baby."

As he reached out to assist me to my feet, I prayed that he wasn't going to take matters into his own hands. Stone was an ex dope boy and had been known to body niggas when he was in that life. I had no doubt that he was capable of killing again, but I didn't want him to risk his freedom for me. When I opened my mouth to utter that to him, nothing came out but a croak. I collapsed back into the chair and cried heavily.

"It's going to be okay," offered Meishelle. She stroked the side of my face gently.

I placed my hand on top of hers, silently thanking her for her compassion.

Hattie Mae assisted Stone in helping me up again. Embracing me tightly to steady my balance, they guided me step-by-step out of the courtroom. When we reached the hallway, Hattie Mae stopped me to wipe the tears that clouded my sight as my eyes tried to adjust and focus on my surroundings.

Quameer and Mariah stopped the conversation with their attorney and stared at me mockingly. Beside me, Stone glared at Quameer. "See me in the streets, bitch ass nigga," he spat.

Quameer maintained a poker face, but I could see fear in his eyes. His pretty ass wanted no parts of a thug like Stone.

My momma cut her eyes at Mariah so hard I thought I saw blood gush from that ho's neck. "You a triflin' bitch," Momma hissed.

"You right about that," Mariah shouted back. "But it takes one to know one. You home-wrecking bitch."

Now her punk ass had done the *most*. I tore away from Stone and Hattie Mae and jumped up in Mariah's face. Who in the fuck did she think she was, talking to my mother like that?

Bop! I punched her dead in the mouth. "Ho, is you crazy?" I railed as a second blow caught her square on the nose and put her on her ass.

"Hold the fuck up," said Quameer. He reached out to stop me from stomping his bitch.

"Nigga, if you put your hands on her I'ma mop this hallway with your punk ass," gritted Stone.

Quameer let his arm fall meekly to his side. By now Mariah was halfway up, but I pounced on her and forced her back down. "Is this what you thought you wanted?" I taunted as I grabbed ahold of her hair with one hand and made a fist with the other.

She reached up to claw at my face, but I pummeled her with blow after blow, punishing her for old and new. Then I banged her head against the marble floor. With each thud I screamed, "You will never be me, bitch!"

Quameer was screaming like a girl. He knew not to try to pull me off of her or Stone and Quincy would've torn into his ass.

"That's enough, sis," my brother finally said. But the sight of blood had turned me animalistic and released all of my rage.

"Hell no!" I screamed. "I'm going to kill this ho!"

Quincy's strength alone wasn't enough to pry me off of her. It took him, Stone, and two officers to restrain me as I punched, kicked, and gouged, trying my best to blind or murder Mariah.

Quameer just stood there looking helpless, watching his bitch lay unconscious as blood oozed from the back of her head.

One of the officers slapped a pair of handcuffs around my wrists and led me away. Quincy and Stone were going off, cussing and hurling threats at the officers' backs. I looked over my shoulder at Quameer and hurled, "Now muthafucka, clean your white trash up off the floor."

Don't Fu#k With My Heart

Chapter 2

After spending the night in jail, I was bonded out early the next morning. Walking out of the giant, green, double doors of Central Lockup, I squinched my eyes against the sun as I walked in step with Quincy to his car.

I took notice of how cock diesel my brother looked walking alongside me. His broad, muscular, build and bald head made him fit the typical description of a bodyguard. He had played football in high school and nothing had changed about his physical appearance since then.

I redirected my attention to a more intense subject once we made it to his car and I saw that Stone wasn't there. "Where is Stone?" I asked immediately, confused by why my man wouldn't be here instead of my brother.

"Your man is good. He wanted to post your bond and pick you up himself, but I assured him that I had everything under control." He tried to ease my mind.

"Whatever," I replied flippantly.

"You hungry?" He changed the subject.

"You must've read my mind," the thought of grits with cheese and liver caused my mouth to water. Less than two minutes away was Anita's Grill, a small diner style restaurant that had the best breakfast in New Orleans. Although my stomach grumbled, I preferred to go home and bathe first. I told Quincy.

"Yeah, that might be a good idea," he agreed, waving his hand in front of his nose.

"Real funny," I replied dryly.

Quincy opened my door and mocked, "Get in, Killa."

I got in and slammed the door, I was not in the mood for any jokes. I fastened my seatbelt and stared out of the window, thinking about everything that happened in the past twenty-four hours.

Quincy continued with the ill-timed humor. "You definitely tore Mariah's ass up yesterday," he chuckled. "I ain't seen that side of you in a while. Welcome back." He held his fist out expecting a pound, but I was not in the joking frame of mind. My baby had been taken away from me so there was nothing to kid about.

I continued to silently stare out of the window as we drove off. Turning the conversation in a serious direction, Quincy said, "You already know your first stop is Hattie Mae's house. Momma is also there waiting for you."

My hunger pangs instantly went away. I slithered down into my seat and sighed heavily. I dreaded going there just like back in my middle school days when I was headed home after getting into trouble. And just because I wanted the ride to be long this time, it seemed to pass by in a split second.

When we pulled up to the curb in front of Hattie Mae's house, I broke my silence. "Please bring me home," I begged him as I began crying.

"Maybe in a few days, but for now you're staying with grandma," Quincy firmly stated.

"I just want to be alone right now," I pleaded.

"No, Krissett. That ain't a good thing for you. If you want Na'Siah back you have to focus on getting yourself together mentally." His tone made it brutally clear that this topic was not up for discussion.

"Yea. You right," I mumbled.

"Right now we need to monitor you. You're likely to do anything. We gotta make sure my nephew comes home on your next court date," he spoke seriously.

24

"I can stay with Stone," I suggested with my head down in my lap.

Ignoring my request, he came around to open my door. Grabbing my hand he said, "Come on. I already brought all your stuff from your house."

As I headed up the porch steps, images of Na'Siah running to the door at the sound of my house keys rattling the locks flashed through my mind. He would stand in the middle of the floor waiting for me to open the door. After seeing it was me, a smile would spread across his face that would let me know he loved me despite anything that happened.

A dizzy spell came over me and I went crashing to the concrete on my knees. Surges of pain shot through every part of my being. Quincy bent down and scooped me into his arms.

"Momma," he called out, "come open the door."

Momma opened the door and instantly panicked. "What's wrong with her?"

"Nothing, Ma, she just lost her balance coming up the stairs," he downplayed the situation.

Quincy carried me inside and gently placed me on the couch. Full of concern, my mother and grandmother took a seat on each side of me.

Hattie Mae was short and stout, with soft, curly, gray hair which she religiously covered with a turban, claiming her head was cold. Her square framed glasses were worn low on her nose, and her soft, pudgy hands possessed the power to heal my soul with a single touch.

Hattie Mae grabbed the small hand mirror that she kept on the coffee table to check her appearance. She held it in front of my face. "Look at this beautiful woman," she said, offering the mirror to me. I continued to stare ahead. She took my hands and placed them around the mirror. "Look at her," she demanded.

Staring at my reflection, I didn't recognize myself. I got up off of the sofa and paced the room. Suddenly, I stopped and hurled the mirror against the wall. "I'm nothing," I cried out.

"Krissett," Momma gasped, slapping her hands against her lap.

I dismissed her response since she never seemed to fully understand me. Growing up, Momma always had to ask a million questions to gain insight into my issues whereas Hattie Mae knew the problem and solution by just looking at me. I cried and begged for my mother to let me live with Hattie Mae, and by the time I was twelve she conceded. She would stop over every day after work to make sure I was okay, but hardly ever invited me to come home. As I came into womanhood, the distance between us widened. Momma saw me as weak while Hattie Mae considered me troubled and longing for the affection that my mother never provided.

I was certain that Momma hadn't ever hated her own reflection. She possessed an abundance of confidence and personality that helped her become one of the top real estate agents in the city of New Orleans.

"Chile, have you lost your mind?" Momma scolded.

Hattie Mae quickly came to my defense. "Leave her alone." With a grunt, she rose from the sofa and gently caressed my face with both of her hands. Looking directly in my eyes she said, "Now if you can't face yourself, how do you expect Na'Siah to see you?" When I didn't respond she continued. "Until you see yourself worthy of love and affection not another soul will. Not even my great grandbaby," she finished, planting a kiss on my forehead.

The room fell silent. Quincy pulled me into a hug. "She's right, ya heard me," he concurred.

I nodded agreeably, but my confidence didn't match the gesture. I had allowed one man after another to destroy my self-esteem and with that I had slipped into a long depression that had cost me my son.

I flopped down on the sofa, totally distraught.

"Baby, why don't you go and lay down while I fix you something to eat? I know you must be starving," said Hattie Mae. She headed for the kitchen without waiting for my response.

Momma patted me on the lap and kissed my cheek, following my grandmother to the kitchen.

I forced myself up on my feet. Quincy was watching me as if he feared that I would collapse to the floor. "I'm okay," I feigned a little smile.

"Love you, sis," he said genuinely.

"Love you more." Wearily, I headed down the hallway to my old room.

The bedroom was still the same as it had been when I first brought Na'Siah home from the hospital, except his baby crib had been converted to a toddler bed that was made up with his favorite cartoon character, Scooby Doo. Pictures of him from each month of his first year adorned the walls. Teddy bears and trains decorated the dresser. I saw a vision of him appear at the door, holding a telephone to his ear. I blinked my eyes and felt the sting of tears. During the time he stayed between my momma's house and Hattie Mae's house, they made sure Na'Siah called me every day. Even in my darkest hours I answered the phone if no more than to hear his voice.

Unconsciously, I reached out for my baby, but he dissipated into the air. Burying my nose into a pair of his pajamas that I found folded up on the dresser, I lay across the bed inhaling his scent. I closed my eyes tightly, hoping I would be shaken awake from this nightmare.

The constant reminders of Na'Siah were driving me insane. The ventilation in the room seemed scarce, triggering dizziness, creating the impression that the room was spinning. The walls contracted, producing the illusion that they would collapse, crushing my body under their weight. I needed to get the fuck out of Hattie Mae's house quick. I wasn't in the frame of mind to drive, but I wouldn't object to being Stone's passenger.

I had met Stone almost a year ago while working at the Winn Dixie grocery store in New Orleans East on Chef Menteur Hwy. It was shortly after I'd been released from one of my seventy-two hour suicide watch episodes. He and his grandmother were regulars in my checkout line. She tried to hook us up, but I wasn't checking for anyone new and made it blatantly clear. My sole focus needed to be on getting myself together. A man could kiss where the sun didn't shine.

In addition, Stone had that D-boy swag and I knew from painful experience that all street niggas in New Orleans were heartbreakers and flat out hos. When I conveyed those sentiments to him one day, he looked at me with puppy dog eyes.

"Now, Ma, why you gotta group me in with those other niggas? What if I told you that all pretty women like yourself got a thousand dudes on ya thong?"

"That wouldn't apply to me because I'm not pretty," I corrected him.

"You're right. My bad," he apologized. *Then he flashed his pearly white teeth and smoothly added, "You're way more than pretty, you're exquisitely beautiful. How's that vocabulary for a street nigga?"*

"It's nothing to get big headed about," I said jokingly as we shared a laugh.

"You wanna talk big heads?" His finger was pointed directly at my forehead.

"Don't do me that," I warned playfully.

That broke the ice between us, but I still refused to give Stone a chance. I had to remain focused and not allow his charismatic ass to break through the barrier I had put up to ward off his kind.

All of that changed a month or so later when I accepted a ride home from Stone. We ended up talking for hours on that ride. I found myself pouring out my troubles to him. He was the very first man that really listened to my problems and before long I looked forward to seeing him every day. Everything was good for the first six months until the females started emerging in drones, playing on my phone all hours of the night or passing by my job while driving his truck.

At one point Quincy even put me on game after finding out they were both fucking the same chick at the same time. He told me he found out during an argument one night. She threw in his face that she was dealing with someone whose money was much longer than his, giving up Stone's name while she was ranting. Stone, however, always hid behind the lame excuse that they were jealous of my First Lady status and upset because he kept it strictly professional with them.

I shook my head at the memories as I called Stone's phone several times, growing furious at receiving the voicemail on the second ring. Nigga was ignoring my calls on purpose. This was the bullshit that made me constantly skeptical of this motherfucker's professed love for me.

An entire sixty damn minutes later he finally decided to grace me with a call back. "Yeah," I greeted him dryly.

"What's good, bae?" He asked, the wind coming through the phone.

"Nothing now," I was throwing on my skirt. I'd decided to just drive my damn self around the block.

"Come on, ma, I was taking care of business. You already know I only have about three more weeks to stack this money so you and I will be straight when I go in."

While I had been fighting for custody of Na'Siah, Stone had been battling the court to maintain his freedom. He'd caught a charge on a routine traffic stop. The wrong color in the wrong neighborhood was a magnet for the police. Fortunately, they only uncovered a few scraps of coke compared to the weight he would have normally had.

About a week before Na'Siah's hearing, his lawyer informed him that there was no way to get off without doing some time. The best deal the District Attorney was willing to offer was a year and a half bid. With good behavior he could serve fifty percent, roughly nine months or less. The ongoing legal case was really providing him an additional excuse to keep in his back pocket as to why he was not available to answer calls.

"Nigga please. Those various, random ass hood rats you're sticking your dick in can't do a damn thing for me." I sighed heavily. "It's the same old shit with you on a different day. I'm about to go out. I'll hit you later."

"I wish you *would* hang up this damn phone," he dared me. "First off, you can chill out with that sticking my shit in another bitch because you know that ain't the deal. Secondly, where the fuck you think you going?" He paused for my response.

"Somewhere away from Hattie Mae's. I can't take this house anymore."

"You better not move. Just get dressed," he demanded. "I'm on my way now."

Throwing my shades on, I hopped into the truck. Stone said the plan was for him to pass by and handle a small issue, Uptown, then we would grab something to eat. Something small to him could last for hours, but whatever was fine with me.

Arriving at the destination he parked in the shade and rolled down my window, permitting the slight spring breeze to flow through the crack. Laying my head back into the seat, listening to the chirping birds, the cool wind tickled my skin, causing goose bumps. In the snap of a finger that changed and the heat and humidity quickly caused me to sweat against the leather seat. It was a good thing Stone had left the keys with me. Leaning over the console to turn on the A/C, my sunglasses fell between his seats.

Digging into the seat, I closed my eyes, struggling for my short, small arms to grip them. "Shit!" I hollered in aggravation. Bringing them up it stunned me that there was a used condom dangling from my lens.

"What the fuck?" I shook my head in disgust. "These simple as hood rats."

All the money this nigga had and she couldn't even get him to bring her to a cheap motel to get fucked. I wondered if it was her looks, her shape, or just whatever, that she had on me that attracted Stone enough to make him want to dick her down. Whatever it was I wanted it and then maybe it could be just about me.

Holding it a little closer to my face, my detective senses kicked into full gear. The condom slightly shimmered from the lubrication and clearly recognizable white semen filled the tip. Searching under the seat, I found the torn gold, extra-large, Magnum wrapper that it came from. Buried under his CD portfolio and a bunch of other junk in the console was the condom box with one of the six missing. The receipt confirmed for me it was the one I discovered. He had just bought them less than three hours ago at a gas station across the canal. That bitch was straight up foul. Unless he was turning hos as tricks, I didn't see how that could equate to business.

My body convulsed uncontrollably as I became enraged. My heart shattered. I slid back into my seat, questioning why I kept finding the same ole type of dude. Tears pressed at my eyes, but I forced them back. I shook my head in denial that I could be so stupid all over again.

Out the gate I had been there. In the first six weeks of meeting him someone pulled up alongside him while he was leaving a transaction and blasted. He suffered a graze wound to his neck and a lodged bullet in his arm. The doctors were afraid removing it would cause him to lose function in his arm so it still remained to the present. I was the one there when he opened his eyes. I spent the nights by his house answering his every beck and call. His boys did a little something, but I made him my priority, only coming after my son.

I almost failed a full college semester missing so many days taking care of him only to find out that everything out of his mouth was a lie. There was no way to fuck up his heart like he had just done mine, because for me to do that he would have had to care. So even though everything in me wanted to do him some serious damage, the fact that any negative behavior from me could make me lose permanent custody of my son made me keep my temper in check.

However, I was still going to get revenge on that bastard, just the kind of revenge that wouldn't get me caught. So with the truck still running, I got out, pulled out the switch blade that I carried like it was medication for my mania, and sliced each and every one of his tires. Then I raised the hood and sliced up anything the blade would go through. I may not have damaged *him*, but his ho mobile was another story. Instead of his vehicle sitting on twenty fours, I had that sucka belly flopping on the hot ass New Orleans concrete. Now let's see who he would be fucking in a broke down car.

With a smile of satisfaction on my face, I embarked on my walk down the street to anywhere, making certain all my discoveries were in plain view on the driver's seat.

Don't Fu#k With My Heart

Chapter 3

Stone made no endeavors to contact me until the week before he was scheduled to accept the deal in court. He texted me with his boy's address in Kingswood, a subdivision in the East, where I could meet him to pick up the stuff I had over at his place. The original plan was that I would stay in his place and maintain it, but after the condom incident Quincy told me to say fuck that nigga.

I was still by Hattie Mae and she was enjoying having me around. I was back in school and agreed to meet him after my last class before picking up Na'Siah. Pulling in front of the house, the lawn was adorned with beautiful palm trees, pink begonias, and other green shrubbery that surrounded a mini fountain. Stone's truck and another car that I assumed belonged to his boy sat in the driveway. After ringing the bell, a nice lady dressed in a two piece, beige, pant suit answered the door.

"You must be Ms. Baptiste," she pleasantly smiled.

"Yes ma'am. Is Gregory here?" I referred to Stone by his legal name.

"He sure is. He's in the dining room area."

"Can you call him for me? I'm in kind of a hurry." Apparently he had something going on and I didn't want to interrupt. It kinda hurt my feelings to know that he had stepped his game up and was fucking with older, professional women now. I wasn't fully over the situation, but as long as me having permanent custody of my son was in jeopardy the last thing I wanted to do was cause a scene or do anything that anybody could use against me in anybody's court of law.

"He asked that you come in while we finish up." She stepped aside to allow me through the door.

Following the lady, I immediately saw that Stone was sitting at a table with the box of my things in the middle of it, signing papers. Getting a good look at what he was signing pissed me off so I grabbed the box and turned to exit the house. That was some low down shit for him to invite me in to see him buying a house. Must have been for another bitch because it did him no good since he was going to prison. It was ok though, I had worse shit than that thrown into my face before, shit like Mariah and Quameer.

"Wait Ms. Baptiste. We're not finished. You're leaving the envelope with the papers I need you to sign."

"Papers?" I raised my brow, questioning her statement.

"Yes, I need your signature for your home." She swung the keys from her finger happily.

I had no idea what she could be talking about. I didn't have a dime to pay for that house. I was in the process of moving back with my grandmother until I finished school. Quincy had been willing to resume taking care of my bills, but I didn't want to be a financial burden to him. He had recently started seriously dating Meishelle and she did enough without taking extra income from her.

"Give me a minute to fill her in please," Stone requested.

"Ok. I'll be outside in the car. Congratulations to you, though," she said as she passed me.

"So you like it?" Stone solicited, still sitting at the table. He didn't wait for an answer, but got up and came toward me. "Look, ma, I couldn't come back empty handed after I fucked up so bad. I had been working on the paper for the house, but had to kick it into overdrive with what's about to go down next week."

"I can't afford this, Stone, much less can I be fucking bought. I'm not that chick." I shook my head, refusing the offer. The house was gorgeous and had already been completely furnished. The long hallway led to three bedrooms and two full bathrooms. The kitchen contained the island that I always wanted and located next to the formal dining room and the living room was a comfortable sized a fire place. There was a nice backyard for Na'Siah to play in and a double car garage.

He explained that the down payment, the house note, and what was needed to be in escrow for the eight or nine months he would be gone was in an account he'd set up for me. The house was move in ready and it was solely in my name, a feat he pulled off by practically breaking a few real estate laws and calling in a few favors from some people he knew. All I would have to take care of were the utilities.

Although I couldn't be bought, this was definitely a once in a lifetime offer. I would be finishing up school soon and hopefully could get on with a company paying a decent salary. My momma had a couple of high end customers she maintained good relationships with that either owned companies or knew people that did, they would certainly be able to help me to achieve that. And being a homeowner, not an apartment renter, would show the judge that I was serious about doing better with my life and taking care of my son. Immediately I changed my mind and decided to accept the house from Stone.

I was sure my family would have something to say, but I signed my name on the line without another thought. They would get over it. Finishing up, Stone asked what my plans were for the day. He wanted to see Na'Siah and take us out to eat before he went in. Deciding to forgive him, I called Quameer to see when we could meet.

"What you mean I can't get him this weekend? I have only seen my son one time in the three weeks since court,

Quameer." I cried, distraught. The hate Quameer displayed was ironic since he had wrong me.

Stone gave me the side eye and motioned for me to put the phone on speaker. I shook my head no, but the stern look on his face told me it was not negotiable.

"Well add this one to the count," Quameer barked. "Mariah has plans to take him to a birthday party so that's a wrap for you."

"Look nigga," Stone interjected. "Bring Na'Siah where we normally pick him up. You a straight ho for handling my girl like this behind her seed."

"Man who the fuck you think you trying to handle? I don't have to do a motherfuckin' thing. Fuck you and that bitch."

"Say brah, I'm going to prison this week so I ain't got shit to lose right now. I suggest you meet me in thirty minutes with Na'Siah or I'm coming to your door."

"Nigga if you that bold, do you. I'll be waiting." The call ended with my phone returning to its screen saver. Quameer suddenly got heart from out of nowhere.

"Let's go," Stone growled.

"Stone, no. Let's just call the lawyer and handle it the right way. I don't need any drama and you about to go in. It's only going to make things worse," I implored him.

"Did you hear what I said to do?" He snarled. His nostrils spewed fire. He clearly didn't share my view point on this.

Fifteen minutes later Stone cocked his nine millimeter, setting up for whatever would go down as we rolled up to Quameer's house. He made me drive so that he could jump out with no interference.

"Stone, look at me baby," I begged. "Please let me at least try to handle this at the door. The last thing we need is this when we go back to court. *Please?*" I entreated him to consider what he was thinking of doing.

"You have one minute. If I have to get out this truck this heat will do any other talking." His eyes spoke that this was no threat, but a promise he would make good on.

As tempting and worthwhile as the offer was to kill Quameer, it would put Stone in jeopardy of more prison time. I walked nervously to do the door, hoping that this would not end in unnecessary bloodshed. Quameer was an ex-dope boy too, but he wasn't truly about that life. His guns had been challenged countless times and each time his bitch ass couldn't be found. Everyone in the streets knew he was a ho deep down and that forced him out the game. If anything, he was the one who had called the police to set Stone up.

Ringing the doorbell, I heard little steps walking to the door. I could see Na'Siah's silhouette with a book bag on his back.

Lord, let this be peaceful, I looked to the heavens for mercy.

Quameer opened the door. "Bitch, tell your nigga don't ever make the mistake of threatening me again. It won't be good for him." He scowled. "I'm no one's ho."

"Mommy!" Na'Siah screamed and ran into my arms. I placed kisses lovingly all over his face.

"I hear you, Quameer. All I want is my son," I snickered at his comments. I'd gotten what I had gone there for and that was all that mattered.

On my way back to the truck, I mouthed thank you to Stone. He winked his eye at me, keeping his hard face to Quameer as he stood in the door. Despite the bullshit, he actually was there more emotionally than I had originally thought. He had my back, I just questioned to what extent.

Don't Fu#k With My Heart

Chapter 4

During the house celebration dinner, the conversation sur-
prisingly flowed freely. After my rubber discovery, I was determined not to deal with Stone anymore. I had decided that
we could be cool and I was willing to hold him down, but
any relationship lay dormant for the moment. Stone had a
captivating personality though, and that easily won me over
and changed my mind.

Next to his looks, his intelligence was remarkable and
sensual as hell. He wasn't the stereotypical dope dealer. He
could hold a conversation about politics, arts, music, finance,
and a countless number of other subjects. By the end of dinner he had persuaded me into another chance with claims
that appeared to be sincere of how much I meant to him and
how much he wanted us to work.

The remainder of the week flew by. Stone not only showered me with gifts, but gave me what I needed the most, attention. He made me feel wanted. Every evening he picked
me up for some us time whether it was a movie, drinks, dinner, or just a ride. Occasionally business arose, but as long
as it wasn't major, he took me with him to handle it. When
his sentence day arrived, I found myself an emotional wreck
outside the courtroom, with him assuring me that everything
would be ok. I tried to put up a strong front, but I whimpered
as his name was called and he stepped forward to receive his
sentence. Leaving court there was an empty void left un-
filled.

He called me every day, but it was a few weeks before I
received my green visitation card in the mail. It would definitely prove to be an interesting visit for him after the new
information that had been brought my way. It aggravated me
to know that I wouldn't have found the out the truth if I

would have followed my first mind and left his ass after I got my house keys. The question about his motive for taking his cell phone's SIM card with him as he turned himself in had been revealed.

I picked up the telephone receiver on the second station as he took his seat on the other side of the bullet proof window that divided us.

"What's up, babe? Looking good." He appeared real happy to see me.

"Thanks, babe. You looking good yourself. How you doing?" I was ready to reveal my findings.

"I'm making it. How are you?"

"I'm good, but I'll be better when you clarify who Keedy is for me?" I looked him square in the eye.

In a hurry to leave he had forgotten to log off his Facebook account. Messages from a chick named Keedy piqued my interest so I decided to look into it further. Messaging her revealed Stone had been dealing with her long before he met me. The same way he took care of me, he took care of her. In addition, she had a key to his apartment and had never seen my stuff there. It dawned on me that that was why stuff I'd left on the bed was always in the back of the closet whenever I returned. Stone demanded obedience so he knew we could never be bold enough to cross him.

"Somebody I was fuckin' with before I committed fully to you." His head hung low and he breathed deeply, comprehending why I was pissed off.

"Fully committed?" I repeated to him. "So we were playing before you came in here then?"

That shit was news to me. There I was thinking the money, time, and attention signified I was the first lady, but in essence I was nothing more than the side chick.

"I'm not going to say that, Ma, but I will admit a nigga was doing him still."

"So when did you leave Keedy alone?"

I knew the answer already, it was a month before he went in, but this would be a test of how honest he would be. He had conveniently forgotten to mention all that when asking for a second chance, and his deceit made me struggle to grasp why I was never good enough for anyone. Fortunately for him his response matched hers. Him and the bitch could have been lying, but I dismissed it as irrelevant since it verifiably occurred before his second chance.

"So tell me then, Stone, why the hell are you with me?" I threw my hands up in exasperation. "You need someone to hold you down? When you were out you were doing you, but now in here you know I'm who you want?" It was time for his ass to come real about what the hell he was doing with me.

"I want you because you have intelligence. You can hold decent conversation, you not out here throwing yourself on a nigga dick for a dollar, and you are loyal and just good people."

"That has yet to be seen. Hear this though. You have seven months to decide what you want to do, but you can't come home playing these games. I ain't doing them anymore with you." My tone was signified by how crucial my words were. I meant what I was saying with every fiber of my being.

"I got you, ma."

Money got tight for a while as I looked for a job after spring graduation. Keeping the utilities paid, my car note, insurance, money on my phone for calls, and other bills proved costly. My momma and my stepfather helped out until I found something. Quincy lost a lot of respect for Stone after the condom incident so I couldn't ask for money that could possibly benefit him. I respected his feelings. He might not intercede, but I believed he hated to see me heart broken.

Quameer still called every weekend with the foolishness about visitation, but he saw them through most times. Quincy volunteered to handle the situation anytime he stepped too far out of line. He had been itching to finish the ass whipping he put on him several years ago.

Back in the day, around the time I realized I was pregnant with Na'Siah, Quincy ran a small chop shop downtown. Quameer desperately wanted street status so he pressed me to ask Quincy to give him a chance, claiming it was to put money in our pockets for the baby. Reluctantly Quincy did it, but only on the strength of me.

A few jobs in, Quameer started running his mouth in the streets to make himself look hard and it got back to the wrong people. Thank heavens the owner had a few cops on the payroll that put him on game because Quameer's dumb ass almost got everyone caught up. Quincy wanted to end his world, but I pleaded on the strength of my unborn baby to let him live. That didn't stop the ass whipping he put on him, though.

Calling the DOC's (Department of Corrections) automated line daily, they had finally calculated Stone's release date to be early January the following year. The lawyer's estimation of the time he would actually serve was pretty accurate. We talked every day and visitation went well on the weekends. Holidays were rough for both of us, though.

Stone was extremely family oriented and being with his family on a holiday was a requirement, from sun up to sun down. A couple of days before the Thanksgiving and Christmas holidays there was a noticeable change in his attitude.

His tone grew sad and I had to pull conversation out of him. I know I couldn't take away the void, but I divided my time between my family and by his grandmother so he could at least get the chance to speak with them on my phone.

Stone's grandmother had blocked his ability to call when he told her he was giving up the game when he came home. The rest of the family had a hundred and one excuses why they couldn't keep money on their phones to accept his calls. When he was on the streets they had no problem opening their hands to take his money, though. At the sight of me his grandmother's face frowned up and she wore a look of contempt for the remainder of the gathering.

His sister, Ja'Riane, told me that she blamed me for him leaving the game. *Kill them with kindness*, I told myself as I plastered a smile brighter than the sun on my face. What was ironic was she was the one who lobbied for me and Stone to be together, always telling him that I was the type of girl he needed. I guess the hood rats she wanted him to leave alone suddenly looked like a much better choice in her eyes.

Astonishing to me was that no other thirst buckets appeared, permitting me and Stone to have peace for the remainder of his bid. Awaiting his release in the cold lobby of Central Lock up, mixed emotions filled me. Up until the night before, Stone claimed he was still sure about wanting only me, but now was the time for actions to be put to his words.

The minute he stepped out the doors, we were going to be on our way to see KEM at the IP Casino in Biloxi. I had paid for the trip upfront out of my last semester's student refund check. I knew a stipulation of being on paper was that he could not leave the state, but we weren't going that far. Besides, his parole officer had given him until Monday to report to the office.

The beige, steel door that had been holding Stone hostage buzzed open at six that morning. With no glass to intercede, I jumped onto him, locking him in with my legs. "Baby wait," he laughed, placing me upright on the floor.

"Boo, you're home!" I screamed, wanting the whole world to know. I planted a huge kiss on his lips.

"Yeah, baby girl, I'm home." He laughed, placing me upright on the floor.

"Let's get out of here. We have plans."

Heading down I-10 East, our first stop was Waffle House for breakfast. They had the nastiest habits ever, but Stone loved them. Next, we hit up the Tanger Outlet malls in Gulfport Mississippi for a few items like Ralph Lauren and Nike. We would hit Saks when we got back so he could get all the way right.

Reaching our destination, we were still early. For upgrading to a Luxury Suite the hotel comped us with an early check in.

Stone gripped a handful of my pussy through the shorts I was wearing, running his tongue along the back of my neck the moment we got to our door. He unfastened the button on my shorts.

"I've been waiting to tear my pussy up," he hissed. I fidgeted with the door key as he inserted his hand inside my lock.

"I've been dreaming of this dick," I cooed. The green light authorized our room entry.

I freed his hand. Entering the room, I dropped my shorts before the door could slam shut, revealing to him that I came completely prepared for the special occasion.

A sneaky grin framed his face. Almost nine months of nothing penetrating me was too damn long. My finger motioned for him to come to me. He charged at me roughly chasing me into the suite. In the bedroom, he knocked me down, pinning me under his body. He nibbled on my neck, moving up to trace my ears with his tongue. His fingers slithered over every segment of my body, pleasing my skin. Stopping at my clit, he rubbed his hands over my lips, ensuring not to make contact with my pearl. His touch moistened my passageway with trickles of vapor. My body quivered in bliss.

"I want you to tattoo your name of the inside of my shit," I gasped.

"Tell me how," he commanded.

"You already know," I continued to lure him in.

Picking me up, he walked me over to the window overlooking the beach. The midday, summer sun harshly beamed down on the waters. My hands loosely hung around Stone's neck. He jammed me against the heated window, hands raised above my head. He inserted his stake, familiarizing himself once again with his hidden treasure. Each prod was slowly breaking through the tight barricade that protected the jewels. With me imploring him to dig deeper, his momentum quickened with each stab. Becoming a gymnast on the balance beam, I extended my legs wide open outwardly to accept every inch of his rod.

Whimpers were all I could utter while our tongues swirled, sharing the passion of the moment. The pressure of his thrusts gliding my back up and down the window cleared the condensation that formed from the heat of the window and our bodies. He hungrily fed on my neck. His passion burned, etching signs of his pleasure on my neck. The exhilaration of a crowd of people stopping to glance up and view our performance thrilled me more. Droplets of dampness accumulated, making the pane too slippery.

Fastening my arms around his neck and my legs around his waist, he used me like a pendulum swinging on and off his shaft. Our skin clapped loudly, sounding off. The whites of my eyes appeared. He had broken into my gut as I shrieked in pleasure. My grip started to loosen from our bodies perspiring. The people in our adjourning rooms would probably call security soon as my hollers could easily be heard.

My arms lost their grip. Throwing my head and body back, I braced my hands on the floor, slanting upwardly onto him. Stone held onto my waist, pile driving into me. Using my arms, I lunged my pussy back at him. My juices gushed, giving his rod a glistening appearance. They spilled over onto my thighs and into my asshole. I was floating high above the sky, in another atmosphere. The intense pinches of gratification that flowed throughout me were incredible.

Sitting on the edge of the bed, he flipped me off the floor onto the top of him. Positioning myself in a squatting formation above his pole I eased down onto the tip of his rod and came back up. With each additional squat I maneuvered further down onto his shaft, clinching and releasing him with my Kegel muscles until I made sure I covered his entire eleven inches.

Slurred sounds was all I could muster, unable to form words. Rotating my hips in a circle, I continued up and down in rapid succession. My clit became stimulated more from rubbing against his skin with each landing. My wetness coated his stomach. He engrossed my breasts into his hands, pinching my nipples with his fingers. I couldn't hold my rain waters any longer. Stone immobilized my feet to the bed and groaned as my downpour flooded his shaft. Then he looked into my eyes and released violently

48

On Saturday, after we'd made it back home, I told Stone we would go to the movies. But before we did that I told him that I needed to pick up an energy bill from his sister. I explained that she was questioning her electric meter working properly and wanted a representative to review her account on Monday.

Stone revealed all thirty-two of his teeth when we got to his sister's house and his family yelled, "Surprise!" Even his grandmother had shown up. He hugged her tightly and whispered something in her ear that made her apparently forgive him by the smile that was suddenly plastered on her face. Noticing me over his shoulder though, that smile was replaced by an immediate scowl.

I went into the back yard and took a seat under a shaded tree to get on my phone or go online or something. His grandmother had been the only one I truly dealt with and since she didn't deal with me anymore, that left me by myself. Realizing I forgot my cell phone, I got up to retrieve it out the car. That's when I saw that some chick was a little too close on Stone for my taste. I knew damn well that nigga didn't have one of his bitches in the building.

"Hey, boo," I announced my presence and awaited the introduction.

"Hey, babe," he replied. "This is Takiesha," he said, looking toward her. "Takiesha, this is my girl, Krissett."

The stare down that followed was intense. I knew her name but it still didn't tell me who she was. Stone broke the silence. "Takiesha was like my little sister back in the day."

My attitude subsided since I now knew what the deal was, but her attitude clearly hadn't gone anywhere as she looked me up and down.

"I'm going to get my cellphone out the car," I informed Stone. "Nice meeting you," I said to Takeisha as I walked off.

"Yeah, uh huh," she replied, waving me off.

Instantly, I stopped. "Excuse me?" My ears must have been deceiving me.

"Baby, just chill. It's good. Just give me a minute," Stone grabbed my wrist.

"Nah. She has a mouth. Let her speak on it." I directed my attention back to her, "Is there some issue you have with me?" Females commonly confused me being pretty and well groomed to mean I would not lay a bitch on her ass.

"And if I do?" She snapped back.

Immediately I forgot all about why I needed to keep my temper and my actions in check. "Oh, we can always address them," I moved closer as Stone stepped between us.

"Let the shit go, Krissett," Stone faced me and spoke seriously.

"Yeah, *Krissett*. It's best that you walk away from this one. You might get your feelings hurt and your ass kicked."

"Bitch, what I can promise you is that *you* could *never* whip my ass."

"Stone, you better let her know." Her tone became an octave too high for my taste, causing his family to look on.

The one thing I couldn't stand was a mouthy bitch. That loud shit didn't scare me, it only pissed me off. I felt like if you had something on your chest we might as well deal with. Word exchange was just wasted energy. I was ready to bust that bitch's ass. And for her to disrespect me for no apparent reason was a huge *hell no* in my book.

"You letting Stone play games with your stupid ass. If I was like a little sister the shit we did would have been incest," she continued to raise her voice.

50

I looked to Stone who stood between us shaking his head. My anger turned toward him as his response was an admittance of guilt to me.

"What the fuck she talking about, Stone?" I directed my questions directly to the source of this beef.

He wouldn't answer.

"Tell her who you used that condom on she found in your truck. Or how about you tell her where you really been during this last week. We only went to the probation officer once, right?"

"Man you fucking trippin' now," he finally spoke up. "You went because Ja'Riane went with me. Ain't nothing going down between us. Don't throw salt to piss my girl off."

I had heard enough. The possibility that this nigga came home and fucked someone else after I stood by his side was enough for me. Everything in me wanted to hit that ho, but it wasn't her doing. It was all on Stone.

"So now you going to front like you wasn't deep see diving in my pussy?" She used her finger and pushed his head aside.

"Go ahead, Takeisha," he warned.

"And if I don't? You know you ain't about to walk away from this shit. You always come back to what you know." She got close in his face.

"Bitch, you sound real stupid. Go ahead with all this frontin' while my girl here."

"Bitch? Nigga you the bitch playing all these games," she bucked.

At those words his face turned into just what his nickname was. He cocked back and punched her in the face as if he was Money Mayweather in the ring, withholding most of his strength, though. Blood spewed from her mouth and she spit the remaining at his feet.

51

"You'll be back," she hollered. "Make sure your ass come correct this time, though."

"Nah," I cut in, "you can have his ass now because I'm done. Make sure your shit is out my house by the end of the weekend."

"Krissett?" He called to me as I walked out of the house. His grandmother waited for me at the door with a smirk of victory on her face. I couldn't do this shit with him anymore.

Chapter 5

"From best friends to sisters," Meishelle said, motioning her glass for a toast in celebration of her engagement to my brother.

We sat across the table from each other at Houston's on St. Charles Avenue three weeks later. We were long overdue for our lunch and celebration date that we tried to do regularly, but often our work schedules conflicted.

"And to our never ending friendship," I replied, clinking my glass with hers.

Meishelle had been so good to me before, but she really became something amazing after the custody battle.

After losing Na'Siah, grooming became my last concern. My hair was always disheveled. Eventually it had to be cut short because it became matted to my head. My shape deteriorated as baggy jogging suits camouflaged my weight gain. Meishelle had quickly stepped in, forcing me to get out of the house daily, by placing me on a routine.

She got up three hours earlier for our four mile morning jog through City Park. During the evening hours I was to be dressed and waiting, even if we were going no further than the Stop Jockin' snowball stand.

It became mandatory that my hair, nails, and toes be done at all times. Spa days were scheduled once every month, unless needed more frequently. In her opinion, appearance was everything. It changed the way a person felt about themselves is what she'd always tell me, and that day I could truthfully say, my girl had been spot on.

"Girl, please, I don't need to be given credit for what a friend is supposed to do," she said, taking a sip of her Merlot.

"You have no idea how much your friendship has meant to me," I sniffled as my emotions threatened to take over.

"Let's talk about something else before I tear up in this place," she dabbed her napkin under her eyes to stop the droplets from falling.

"Okay," I agreed. "You ready to formally become a part of my family, Mrs. Baptiste?"

"Yes. Of all the men in the world, I still can't believe that I ended up with Quincy." Meishelle shook her head from side to side.

"Me either. Y'all couldn't stand each other when we were teenagers," I laughed.

"Pretty much, but we aren't teenagers anymore, are we?" She held her hand out and wiggled her fingers. The sunlight from our window seat hit the diamond and caused light to shine all over our table.

I held my hand up to cover my eyes. "Girl, please put that down. You're going to put my eyes out with that sparkle."

"I know right," she giggled, flashing it one last time.

I reached over the table and took her hand to get a closer look at the ring. The two carat, cushion cut, platinum diamond ring was gorgeous. The center cut and band were surrounded by smaller diamonds, heightening the glistening of the jewel.

"I can't believe how big the stone is," I said, still admiring it. "You never need to question if my brother loves you, sportin' a rock like that."

Before she could respond, the waitress came over to take our order. Meishelle ordered the Chicago style spinach dip, jumbo lump crab cakes with coleslaw, and apple walnut cobbler. I asked for the Grilled Chicken Caesar with mixed greens and vinaigrette dressing.

"I can't figure you out," she shook her head at me as we handed the waitress our menus.

"What?" I asked bewildered.

"You have a shape bitches would kill for, a fat ass, thick hips, and nice thighs, but you eat like a fuckin' bird."

"Girl, please, we can't all be thin, Broom Stick." Quincy had given Meishelle that nickname to tease her petite and slim frame.

"Whatever," she waved her hand, dismissing my comment. "You deserve to loosen up a little bit. When was the last time we were able to do this? You should eat whatever you want and drink like a fish."

"I'm not paying you any mind. This wine is enough," I laughed. "I have a job to return to when we leave here. I not trying to get fired from acting a plum fool. Thank you."

"You better not. Because if you have to depend on Stone's scandalous ass to support you, you will be assed out," she slick criticized.

I rolled my eyes at her comment. Meishelle couldn't stand my boo.

I truly believed that I had earned his loyalty. "No ma'am, Stone would never turn his back on me," I defended him to Meishelle. "Secondly, when he was in the game I wanted for nothing," I added, letting her know not to come for him.

"Like that shit with Keedy or Takeisha? What do you call that? Stone has definitely done more than his share of untrustworthy foolishness. You give your all and they kick you in your ass. First Hollow, then Quameer, and now Stone."

After I'd calmed down from the incident at the party, I realized that trick Takeisha was lying. When I thought about what she'd said, I figured out that she could have only gone with Stone to his probation officer that one time with Ja'Riane like he'd said because I went with him every other time. I couldn't honestly account for the other days she claimed to have been with him, but a bitch that lied about one could lie about all.

Stone came clean about her being the chick involved in the condom incident, but swore that was it. Ja'Riane corroborated my suspicions that her girl was lying about everything that she said took place since Stone had been home. She was pissed because she wanted more of a relationship but Stone told her all he wanted was a friendship. I figured his no good ass grandmother had something to do with it, especially after remembering the smirk on her face.

I randomly checked our cell phone account just to make sure everything was in order with his call log. Most numbers I recognized immediately and if I didn't, I blocked my number from showing and called them. None of the voices yet had belonged to a female.

"Quameer and Hollow, I'll give you those, but since Stone and I agreed to start over there has been nothing. However, let me point out, it was you who introduced me to Hollow so the decisions weren't all on me," I replied, pointing my finger at her.

"Good point, I guess," she sighed. "If you're happy I'll just leave it be."

As usual my girl had my back, but on this one she couldn't speak on. When she and Quincy first started dating, it brought plenty drama my way, having to deal with the scalawags that Quincy wasn't ready to give up. He couldn't hit a woman, but I had no trouble with beating a bitch, especially for Meishelle's happiness. When he slowly started to eliminate them, I was glad someone was finally showing him one woman could be better than a million.

"So have you and my brother set a date for the wedding?" I attempted to lighten the mood again.

"Yep, I want a summer wedding, no later than August. That gives you six months to get your maid of honor shape together." She mimicked quotation marks with her hands.

"That's more than enough time."

We sat there discussing the plans and the guest list, but in the back of my mind I couldn't help wondering if Meishelle knew something about Stone since he had been home, especially since she was being so hard on him. But I decided to ignore those unwanted thoughts. She *was* my bestie, but I wasn't going to start doubting my man based on her intuition, or her plain old dislike for him.

Don't Fu#k With My Heart

Chapter 6

The waitress walked up and placed Meishelle's appetizer on the table.

"This definitely isn't a good start to getting my shape wedding ready," I confessed, holding up a tortilla chip full of dip. Just as I placed the chip inside my mouth, my phone rang. "Oh, shit!" I shouted, frantically searching my purse in the chair next to me. It was probably my boss calling me about our evening meeting. I had more business meetings than I cared for, being in management on my job.

Immediately upon graduation I had landed a job with Entergy, the power company in New Orleans. Because of my degree in business, a management position had been practically handed to me. Digging the phone from the bottom of my extra-large, monogrammed, MCM leather handbag, I grasped it and held it up to my ear, just as the caller was hanging up. Reviewing my call log, I saw the words blocked ID.

Meishelle noticed the look of disgust on my face. "Who was it?"

"I'll be damned if I know. Someone called from a restricted number so it couldn't have been anybody special." I started to return the phone back inside of my purse, but before I let it go from my hand it rang again, displaying the same unknown caller ID. "I don't know who the fuck it is, but if it ain't about money it's gon' be a problem," I frowned.

"Stay calm," Meishelle cautioned, barely above a whisper.

I pressed the answer button on the screen. "This is Krissett," I answered sweetly, in a professional voice just in case it was my job.

"Krissett?" He said.

I squeezed my eyes together tightly, recognizing my son's father's voice. I wasn't in the mood for him and his bullshit. "What, Quameer?" I snapped.

"You have a sec' for me to holla at you?" He asked politely.

I wrinkled my forehead. "Is this something that can wait? I wanna stay in the good mood I'm in, so if this involves any type of bullshit, then no, I don't have time." Quameer could fuck my day up in a split second.

Once upon a time Quameer had been my high school sweetheart. The sun, moon, and stars rose with him. He was the first boy I was allowed to officially date or call my boyfriend. I met him when I transferred to John McDonogh Senior High in my junior year. From the time we met two months into the school year, we became inseparable.

Before and after school he would get off the bus at my stop to make sure I got home. He walked me to each one of my classes and lunchtime we met in the backyard. I had few friends since all the girls were pissed that I had gotten him. On Valentine's Day they boiled with jealously at the teddy bear, card, and balloons he would bring. We were so inseparable that even on holidays we were together, and our parents took turns bringing us to each other's homes.

Before he left, our apartment walls had been decorated with our happy history, pictures from our homecomings, junior prom, senior prom where he stunned everyone and proposed to me after being elected Prom King. On each picture, genuine smiles of happiness were on our faces. Each month we took family photos after Na'Siah was born so we would always remember how happy we were. The photographer never had to do much to get a smile out of Na'Siah and he added to the love we already shared. Now, two bitches later, he was with Mariah and I wished someone would put a bullet through the back of his head after all he had put me through.

"Well, not really," Quameer answered as he cleared his throat, "I'm calling about my boy."

"I figured that much because otherwise you would have no business calling me," I stressed. "In addition, why you are calling my phone from a private number?" I was already becoming agitated with the way this conversation was going.

"I'm hitting you from Mariah's phone. She doesn't want you to have her number."

"Tell that simple bitch tricks are for kids. I wouldn't give that ho the satisfaction," I hissed.

The patrons sitting at the next table looked over at me, then quickly looked away. *Nosy asses.* I slid out of my chair, motioning to Meishelle with my head that I was going to step outside.

"What's the deal? You talking or not?" Quameer asked.

"Since there's never going to be a good time for you to fuck up my day, I guess now is fine."

Pushing the door of the restaurant open, I quickly walked toward the end of the parking lot. "How can I help you, Quameer?" I asked through pursed lips.

"I'm calling about some money for Na'Siah."

"Money. For what this time?" I asked brashly as I held my nails in the air, admiring the lilac purple hue.

I made a promise to myself that I would not feed into any of his negative energy and give him anything to take to court against me. I gazed to the sky questioning God why, of all people, He gave me a baby with that piece of shit for a father. Lately his unemployed ass would call claiming Na'Siah necessitated money for a field trip, promotional exercise, whatever, but would never provide enough details so I could attend. I didn't recall the judgment including child support payments, but I would send the money anyway because I wanted my son to have what he needed.

Quameer said, "Since your attitude is so nasty I'm not explaining shit to you, ya heard me. But you can't get Na'siah this weekend."

"Why the fuck not?" I snapped. "You pull this same bullshit every week."

"Who the fuck are you talking to?" He used the bass in his voice to invoke fear, but my days of being scared of him were long past. Quameer had proven that he was bitch-made. Whenever he encountered Stone, he shook like a stripper. There was no way I would allow him to intimidate me like he'd done when we were together. "Nigga, you're over there putting on a show for that ho, but your pussy is bigger than hers. I swear if you keep pulling this shit with Na'Siah I'm going to get you fucked up," I threatened.

Quameer shot a slick remark back at me and before long we were cussing each other from A to Z. I was all kinds of crazy bitches and I called him every type of pussy ass nigga my tongue could formulate.

"I'm sick of that dumb ho," Mariah blared in the background. "Give me the fuckin' phone. That bitch gone learn today."

If I hadn't been so angry, Mariah's remark would've been hilarious. What was I going to learn when it was *she* who had worn the ass whopping when we tangoed. She came on the phone talking like she needed a refill.

"Mariah, don't even try to come for me," I promptly cut her off. "You know I don't have an issue with spankin' that ass."

"Any day, bitch!" she blasted.

"Girl, get the fuck out of here," I chuckled. "You should still have nightmares from the last time I *Chris Tuckered* your ass."

"Oh, you can bet I'll be ready for you next time. I promise you I'm going to make you respect me."

"Tuh! There ain't nothin' to respect about a bitch who came behind me tryna take my life. How long will you be chasing a dream that will never come true?"

"Bitch, bye. I never have and never will want to be you. What is there to want? Who would want to be a suicidal ho always trying to off herself? Don't get it twisted, you chasin' my life, bitch. You want Quameer and Na'Siah all back together so bad it's amusing to watch," she finished as if she had just checked me.

"You can't be serious," I shuttered at the thought of Quameer ever attempting to return to me. "You been fuckin' delusional since we were little. The baby is mine you dumb ho. You ain't nothin' but a fill-in. Get your own fuckin' life, you triflin' bitch."

"Fuck you, Krissett!"

"Nah, Mariah. Why don't you fuck your man and have your own baby? Oh, wait, my bad, your ruined ass can't have no babies 'cause you tryna fuck everything of mine and then some, slut. Those private dick suckin' dances in the V.I.P. room of the strip club came with consequences, huh ho?" I said, laughing hysterically.

"Bitch, you can laugh now, but I'll have the last laugh when they take Na'Siah away from your stank ass for good. Why don't you have a successful suicide attempt? We could be taking our family vacations with the insurance money."

"You petty, bitch. We all need something to hope for. If you put that kind of faith into your ruined womb, your wish just might come true," I said, getting furious at her last comment. I had entertained them long enough, now it was time to end the call. "Make sure y'all have my baby together on Thursday evening."

Not waiting for her to reply, I disconnected the call as I tried to calm my nerves. *Checkmate bitches,* I thought with a slight smirk. I'm sure the silence let her know the conversation was over.

Meishelle tried to force a smile on her face when I rejoined her. She asked me if everything was okay when she heard me ask the waitress to have my food put into boxes and to bring the check.

Brushing the situation off I said, "Everything is fine. Quameer is trying to pull his usual bull with Na'Siah this weekend, but it's not going to happen. And you already know Mariah's silly ass is always trying to make her presence felt."

Meishelle shook her head in dismay, then offered support as usual. "Everything will be okay. I'm so sorry about the way Quameer is treating you. Na'Siah will be back home where he belongs, don't worry."

"I sure hope you're right. This has been the longest year of my life. Sometimes it feels like I'll never regain custody," my voice turned sad.

"You will. Just don't give up."

"Never," I said sincerely.

The waitress appeared with the bill and food just as I'd asked. I couldn't wait to get out of there. *Leave it to Quameer to fuck up a good day*, I thought to myself as I pulled out my card to pay for the food.

Meishelle grabbed the check so fast I couldn't even see the total. "I wish you would even try it," she said.

I smiled and handed over my American Express card, anyway.

Meishelle rolled her eyes and laughed, "You always do that shit with your slick ass. Next time I'm going to get the check while you're in the bathroom or something."

I made a funny face at her and exclaimed, "Now what?"

"Nothing," she said, shaking her head.

While we waited for the waitress, we talked about getting together to do some planning for the wedding. I made sure to finish my glass of wine. I needed something to relax my nerves so I could finish my work day. I thought to myself, *I'll definitely be hitting the gym later to relieve some of this stress.*

When the waitress returned with my credit card we gathered up our doggie bags and our purses and headed for the door, chatting as we walked.

Once outside, I hugged Meishelle tightly and said, "I'm so sorry I let him ruin our celebration lunch."

"Girl, please," she said, hugging me tighter. "I'm just happy we can have these lunch dates like we used to."

"I am too. Love you, chick," I said.

"Love you, too. Make sure you call me later."

"Okay," I promised as I watched her climb into her car and pull off, smiling the entire time.

Quincy truly had himself a winner.

Don't Fu#k With My Heart

Chapter 7

Jumping into my bowling ball blue Mustang G2, I slipped on my black, oversized, rectangular Dior sunglasses. The engine purred as I turned the key in the ignition. After allowing my convertible top to retract, I felt the sun kiss my skin. It was late February, but the weather felt like early summer.

As I drove off with the wind in my hair, Anita Baker's soulful voice blared from my iPod. I wet my lips and hummed along to her song, *No One in the World.*

Cruising down the now empty avenue, Mardi Gras beads draped the trees and balconies. A few weeks ago it had been bustling with residents and tourists who hollered out, "Throw me something mister," at the float riders who paraded the streets.

Heading toward the Central Business District, I sank my body into the tan fabric seats and pushed everything to the back of my mind.

It took me about twenty minutes to get back to the office. Since I would be away from my phone for a while, I made sure to check it after parking. I had two missed calls and five emails from my boss. He seemed to be worried that I would miss my evening meetings. The man acted like he couldn't do anything without me.

Being the manager of customer service allowed me a flexible schedule while bringing home six figures. I could dart out to lunch whenever I felt like it and stay gone as long as I wanted to. As long as I got my work done, no one bothered me if I returned to the office later than usual. Twisting the conference room door, I inhaled and plastered my pleasant, professional face on. "Only four more hours," I regretfully mumbled to myself.

***

As soon as the meetings were finished, I grabbed my bags and headed to the parking garage. I was anxious to hit the gym and burn off some calories and some stress. The moment I was safely in traffic, I dialed Stone's number. The phone rang loudly through the speakers.

"Hey, boo," I said as soon as he answered.

"What's good, baby girl?"

"Nothing much, on my way to the gym to work off some of this tension, today was kinda rough."

"Damn. It was like that, huh? What happened?" He inquired. I loved that he always took the time to listen to me gripe.

"Quameer called me with the usual bull."

"What that nigga say?"

"Tryna charge me for my visitation this weekend."

"I'm gettin' real, real tired of that dude thinkin' he can play games with you and use Na'Siah as a pawn. I had plans for me and lil' man to go catch a basketball game."

Smiling I said, "Aww, baby. That's so sweet. He'll definitely like that."

"Yeah, you know that's my boy. I got y'all."

"I never doubt that, baby. What you feel like eating tonight? I can pick something up on my way in."

"Someone called in so I'm working my second job tonight, but how about we catch a movie? We can spend some time together and get your mind back on us," he offered.

Stone did landscaping by day and security at night. Neither job earned him a fraction of what he used to make in the streets, but I was perfectly content with his income. At least I didn't have to worry about him going back to prison. At first Stone wasn't really feeling the legit life, but it was either that or I was walking away. He may have been able to handle another prison bid, but I damn sure couldn't.

My income allowed us to live comfortably and I gave him free reign over our finances so he could handle responsibilities as close to the same way he always had. He respected that. In return, he was so attentive to my needs and I adored him for it. Every night that he wasn't working we did something together, even if it was taking a walk on the levee to talk. On Monday's or Wednesday's we'd get thirty-two ounce daiquiris, pop some popcorn and have movie night. He was definitely working on my insecurities by assuring me it was only me in his world.

"You comin' through to the job tonight?" He asked.

"Of course, after the gym. I'll go home, get fresh, and then come by there."

"Oh, yeah? Well, you know I like that shit fresh and tight," he remarked sexily.

"What about wet?" I came to a stop at a traffic light and squeezed my thighs together.

"That's my job, ya heard me."

"Yea, I heard you. But I'm tryna *feel* you," I let it be known. "Are you workin' alone?" I cooed naughtily.

"You know the deal. Just bring my shit and I promise you'll feel me." I could hear the lust in his voice.

Honking horns alerted me that the light had turned green. I shot my middle finger in the air and slowly pulled off as I continued talking to my baby. By the time I neared the gym, Stone had my kitty throbbing.

Pulling up to the building, I took a few deep breaths to calm the tingling between my thighs. Once kitty stopped purring, I used my mirror to pull my hair into a bun on top

of my head. Taking those Hair Finity pills had my hair almost back to its original length. "Baby, I made it here. I'm
about to go get it in for about an hour," I informed my man.

"A'ight. Keep that body tight for me. Just like that
pussy."

"Always. I'll call you before I head that way. Love you."

"Love you, too."

*　*　*

The half-moon graced the sky just as I reached my house.
The workout granted me time to burn off the day's frustration. Checking the time on the cable box, I saw that I still
had time to prepare for Stone.

I sat my keys on the dining room table and went straight
to the bedroom. Stripping out of my sweaty gym clothes, I
went over to my walk-in closet in search of potential outfits.
Fiddling through my skirts and dresses section, nothing
would suffice for the impression I wanted to make, so I decided to go ahead with my bath.

Decorating the edge of the tub with lighted, scented,
strawberry candles, I poured my liquid bubbles inside the Jacuzzi tub and then stepped in. The warm water seeped into
my pores and removed all of the tension out of my muscles.
I laid my head on the back of the pillow and closed my eyes.

My mind drifted to Na'Siah. I visualized when I would
boggle him down with a million and one questions about
how his day at school had gone. I could hear him telling me
which letter he'd learned, reciting his colors, and all about
what his friends had done.

I ran my hand along the edge of the tub until I found my
phone. I sighed as I picked it up and dialed Quameer's number. The phone rang two times before I was sent to

voicemail. I tried one more time before giving up. I couldn't stand that reckless son-of-a-bitch. He could call me weekly with foolishness about my visitation, but refused to let my baby tell me good night.

It dumbfounded me that this had been the very mutha-fucka who begged me not to have an abortion when he found out I was pregnant. He professed to have endless love for me and begged me to let us become a family. Like a fool I had given in to his pleas and his pitiful ass had been fucking over my heart ever since our junior year of high school. Feeling the temperature of the water starting to drop, I decided it was time to get out of the tub and get myself dressed and ready.

Making my way out of the bathroom, I sauntered to Na'Siah's bedroom. His toys were still scattered all over the floor just like he'd left them last weekend, but I had made his bed.

I smiled down at the Saints comforter and pillows. They were his favorite team just like his mommy's. I could hear his little feet running through the house screaming, *"Mommy, mommy!"*

I fought back the urge to take the Somas I had slipped out of Hattie Mae's pill bottle a month ago when I had taken her to the emergency room to have her finger stitched up. The thought of her Somas mixing with the Lithium I had been prescribed for my mania and took on a daily basis made my hand twitch as a voice inside my head urged me to pop a pill. The opiate would provide a temporary euphoria along with an easy escape from the harsh reality Quameer had cre-ated for me.

No, you don't need that, I told myself. Remembering that I would get another date for family court real soon and not have to deal with Quameer like that anymore, I suppressed the desire to get high. The top priority on my agenda was to get my baby back home. Nothing was more important.

Feeling proud of myself for exercising control, I laid across Na'Siah's bed and fell asleep hugging his pillow and inhaling his scent.

Chapter 8

When I woke from my nap it was time to get ready for the other love of my life. I still hadn't decided what I would wear yet. Possibilities continued to run through my mind as I oiled my body. The one thing I was certain of was that it had to be sexy and over the top for him. The notion that my boo never knew what to expect in the bedroom caused by pussy to pulse. Then the perfect ensemble came to mind.

Looking through the drawer, I picked out my navy blue G-string and a pair of iridescent boy shorts. I went to the closet and grabbed the Richard Sherman Seattle Seahawks jersey. I had just bought the outfit last week because he couldn't stand them. His reaction would be priceless. Like the rest of my family, he bled black and gold.

I pulled the string up just a bit under the edge of the shorts so it was noticeable. The boy shorts came right above my ass cheeks, so a little cheek was left hanging out. The navy blue stilettos made it appear as if they rose a little more. I folded the jersey up to where my naval ring could be seen and knotted the excess in the back, securing it with a rubber band. I pulled my hair into a bun so my face would be seen clearly. The only make up I added was some light eyeliner to bring out my hazel eyes. I walked over to the mirror to check my look and blew a kiss of satisfaction at my reflection. I hoped he was ready.

Grabbing my duffle bag with my necessities, I headed out of the door. Once in the car, I grabbed my nine mill out the duffle bag and sat it on the side of my seat. I didn't go anywhere without it in the city, including walking into Stone's job, a nigga would carjack you at a red light in a minute. Settling in, I hit Stone up.

"What's good with you, shorty?" Stone greeted me.

"Nothing, boo. Just letting you know I'm on my way. You need anything?"

"Nah, I got everything I need here, except ya' sexy ass. Come bring me my shit."

I was relieved because had I stopped to get anything I would've definitely caused a major car pileup. "I don't know if you ready for me tonight," I teased him.

"Oh, no?" I could imagine the wheels spinning in his head as he tried to guess what I might have in store for that ass.

"Yeah, I got some real freaky shit planned, baby. You ready for some football?" I asked.

"Football, huh?"

After the day I had, I needed to be fucked real hard. The love making, toe curling sex could wait for another day.

"Yep, not flag or touch either. I'm talking all pro, tackling NFL football."

"Aww shit, that's what's up. Let me go make these rounds real quick and check the building before you get here."

"Okay, baby. I'll see you in a few."

"Bet that."

I disconnected the call and dropped my phone on my lap. "I'm that chick," I said out loud and wiggled in my seat.

I searched through my iPod for a song that would complement my mood. Looking through the selections, I found *Drop It Low,* and bobbed my head as I sang along.

"Yeah boy, you like that. I can tell that you like that. Yeah boy, you love it when my booty goes..... boom-ba-ba-boom, ba-boom, ba-boom, boom. Drop it low girl, drop it drop it low girl, drop it drop it low girl..."

That was definitely my intention. I pressed my foot down on the gas pedal and in no time at all I was pulling up to Stone's job.

Unlocking my phone, I hit him with a quick text.

12:02 a.m.: I'm outside, you know where to be

I got out of the car and slowly walked through the parking lot to make him sweat just a little while longer. Just as I put my hand on the door knob, my phone lit up.

12:04 a.m.: Where you at?

Opening up the door, I immediately saw that the office was empty. The medium sized space sat at the front entrance of the warehouse gate. It contained a two piece desk that was near a sectional sofa. On one end was a TV that gave several camera views of the property, a few spaces over there was a computer that Stone utilized to log his inspections of different areas during the night. Right behind the desk and chair was a love seat.

Four poles outside contained lights that pointed in opposite directions, away from the shack. The darkness would conceal us if anyone pulled up, but that wouldn't be a problem for another few hours. I smirked as I considered using that to my advantage. I stepped out of the boy shorts and placed them next to me on top of the desk. Before sitting the phone down, I sent another quick text.

12:07 a.m.: You coming of out the locker room? It's game time!

Opening my overnight bag, my silver bullet beckoned to be used. Leaning onto the front edge of the desk, I spread my legs into a wide V. Intensely, I peered at the door and pinched my nipples, causing my breasts to tingle. Taking them into my hands, I raised them to my mouth and stroked them lightly with my tongue. The G-string became moist as my fountain trickled.

The bullet vibrated violently on high speed. Restraining it against my clit with my left hand, I entered my burrow using my two right fingers. Massaging my inner walls, my faucet began overflowing and the clear liquid shimmered as I slid them in and out. I threw my head back from the shock waves that pulsated through my vessel. Speeding up my pace, moans escaped my lips. The pressure that fostered was indescribable. My panting grew increasingly louder as I lost control. My head came back to attention as the door creaked.

Stone stood in the doorway with arms folded across his chest and a boot in his mouth. He knew the hard core look drove me wild. His dreads were neatly braided into a single braid going toward the back of his head. The sweaty undershirt clung to his six pack through the unbuttoned uniform shirt he wore. His pants bulged out at the crotch, a sign of his enjoyment. The man was the epitome of sexiness.

Breaking our stare, he ridiculed the Seahawks' cornerback jersey and said, "Don't stop, nothing more I'd rather see than the sea birds fuck themselves." His eyes roamed the remainder of the jersey, focusing on where his primary interest lay. Getting on top of the desk to give him a better view, I spread my knees, rapidly plunging my fingers in and out of my pussy, looking as though I was horseback riding. "I said I want them to fuck each other," he commanded, "Them two fingers ain't doing nothin'."

Ramming four of them inside me, I discovered more of my tunnel. Surges of bliss ran through my body as I hit bottom and found my secret spot. Squishing sounds came from my insides like a water bottle being shaken up.

"Come on, baby, make that shit talk to me," he said, lust filling his vocals.

"This feels so good. I can't hold it!" I screamed out, letting my pleasure be heard.

"Release that shit, Ma."

A few seconds later liquid squirted from between my thighs and my body shook fiercely. "Oh, shit!" I panted as Stone walked over and lay soft, sensual kisses on my lips.

Getting my balance back, I put two fingers back inside of my pussy and brought them back out with thick, clear cum dripping from them.

"You don't at least want to taste the competition and see?" Putting one finger in my mouth, I offered the rest of my saturation to him.

"Umm," he said taking them in. "I'm sorry, baby, but I'ma have to bust that ass."

Using my other hand, I unbuttoned his pants. Switching places with him on the desk, I slipped down to the floor. "You deferred the kick off until the second half. The ball is mine," I said seductively. Gazing up at him from my knees, I tasted his balls one at a time.

I used my saliva as lotion on his shaft and then I rubbed in the moisture with my hands. Licking around the head, I opened my mouth wider to conquer more of his eleven inches. One hand stroked up and down his rod while the other fondled his balls.

"Shit, Krissett. What the fuck you doin'?" He tightly gripped the back my head.

I came off of it for a minute to skeet more of my oral juices onto him. "Bustin' that ass," I replied slowly.

Slurping his rod, my head moved feverishly back and forth as I tried to extract the cream from his chocolate cone. Activating my gag reflexes, both hands glided up and down him with spit running off of them as they became drenched.

"Damn, girl," he growled, trying to pull me up, but I made myself likened to dead weight and anchored myself to the floor. "Fuck," he groaned as his legs twitched the moment he rewarded me. The salty cream coated my throat. I slowly continued to draw him in and out making sure not a drop was wasted. His legs began to give out and he slid off of the desk. He stood up trying to regain some strength. "Shit, girl. You *did* that." I allowed him to pull me into his arms for a minute. "Who you reppin?" He asked deviously.

"Seattle, baby, the twenty-fifth man all day, every day."

"Oh, yeah?" His brow questioned me.

"We spanked that ass in the first quarter," I bragged. Walking to the leather loveseat, I untied the knot in the back of the jersey. "Second quarter, you ready to fuck the competition into halftime?" Lifting it over my head and throwing it to the floor, I turned around to face him.

"No doubt," he said, walking over to me, caressing himself back to full attention.

"So how you want to hand it to 'em?"

His eyes told me he wanted to *dig in that ass*. Mounting the sofa on both knees and burying my head in the back sofa cushion, I spread each of my ass cheeks with both hands.

Grinning wickedly he said, "Since they showed me no mercy in the first quarter, I'm 'bout to punish that ass in the second."

Lubricating my ass with KY, I relaxed my muscles, waiting for the game clock to resume. He slowly eased the head in. Inch by inch, he continued to unlock my tightness. My muscles contracted from the force. Once he unbolted the final latch, my eyes rolled into the back of my head. I inserted my bullet, ready for the play to begin. It caused an instant down pour of rain from the inside of my cave.

I turned around, looked him dead in the eye and mouthed, "Show no mercy."

He nodded and initiated the play. Turning the bullet on, he pounded into my ass deeper and deeper. My breasts unmercifully beat against each other from the force. The sting of them colliding added to the intensity.

"Y'all don't know shit about defense," he taunted.

I opened my mouth to respond, but nothing would come out. The pain from his thrusts along with the tremors of pleasure in my fissure drove me insane. He was gaining yards with each thrust, easing closer to the goal line with each push.

"Whose team is the best?" He pulled my bun loose, wrapping my hair into his fist.

"Check the scoreboard," I managed to get out through heavy breaths.

Pain ran down my spine as he tugged harder. I wasn't ready for it to end. He was definitely attempting to get the victory.

Extraordinary delight streamed through my veins. "Your team ain't shit. You can't even get a score!" I screamed out.

"Watch how quick we can get it in," he whispered in my ear as he yanked my head back. He rammed in and out of me with all his strength, making sure none of his dick was left bare.

"Fuck, I can't believe I'm letting you come back on me." Freeing my head, I buried my face in the sofa cushion, making sure all of me was accessible.

"Ain't no bitch in us, baby. We don't bow down to nobody."

"Except us, we still up, nigga," I pushed my ass back into him.

"Oh, yeah," he said. "Watch this move." Leaning his weight on me, he reached around the front of my body and stuck his fingers inside my pussy, driving the bullet further inside. Shivers ran down my spine, my body began to shake, and an overwhelming feeling grew inside of my stomach. I started seeing stars as if I'd been knocked out during a fight. I was lifted to a new realm of pleasure and it became clear to me I wasn't going to win this quarter of the game. The room started spinning as I became light-headed from ecstasy. "Whose team is the best?" he asked, reaching the end zone.

"*Yours!*" I screeched as my cum hydrant sprayed, determined to put out the fire.

Hearing that one word from me sent him into orgasmic overtime and his whole body stiffened as he gushed his victory cream inside of me. Too exhausted to do anything else, he pulled out and fell onto my back as sweat from his forehead dripped across my skin.

"I had no idea y'all could play like that after the blowout lead we had." By now, I had stretched out on the sofa.

"Counting us out was the mistake," he said as he lay down behind me. "We always have a backup."

After halftime, Stone proceeded to tear me up in all kinds of positions on the field. I couldn't handle overtime so I forfeited the game. He had knocked every bit of tension out of me. Good thing there was about two hours left before I had to leave. I needed a nap to rejuvenate myself for the ride home.

Wrapped in his arms, lying on the sofa, our labored breathing calmed a bit.

Stone had thus far lived up to his promise when he came home. He had made spending time with me first and foremost. Each week we had scheduled date nights and the nights he worked always ended on this sofa. He made me feel wanted and desired inside and outside of the bedroom. It was the little things like the calls throughout the day, the texts, the occasional gifts that told me I was on his mind. I no longer questioned what was wrong with me and why I couldn't find a good man of my own. My self-image became clearer each day.

Hollow, Quameer, and a few other relationships had demolished my belief that any man wanted a decent woman. Before I met Stone, I had vowed not to give my heart to any other man. Passing Stone up would have the biggest mistake of my life.

"I been thinking," he said, breaking into my thoughts. "You know I love you and Na'Siah, right?" My body became powerless as I inhaled deeply. I'd heard this shit a million times before. It usually followed with bullshit about needing space or time I closed my eyes tightly, praying he was different and that I'd made the right decision in trusting him with my heart. He lightly nudged me, "Baby, you okay?"

"Yeah, I'm okay. What's up?" I asked, fearful of his answer.

"Well, I been thinking it's time me, you, and Na'Siah become a family," he proposed.

"What do you mean? In my mind we already are," I replied.

"I mean officially. I want you to have my last name and I want to put my own bun in your oven."

"You sure about that?" I asked as I turned my body to look him in his eyes. I believed that if a muthafucka could look you in the eyes and lie, he had absolutely no love for you. "I know I just put it on you good and all, but you don't owe me your last name as payment for this nookie," I said, laughing to conceal my nervousness.

Stone didn't crack a smile. Instead his eyes became very serious. "Krissett, I'm not playing, shorty." He spoke with sincerity. "Good pussy might earn a bracelet, but only a good heart and the type of loyalty you've shown me can earn a ring. You've stuck by a nigga when those I thought were down left a nigga hanging. You've proved your love and by putting a ring on your finger I hope to prove mine."

His words touched me, but I didn't want him to feel obligated to marry me because I had held him down. I replied, "Seriously, boo, I'm good with what we have now. You don't have to make me your wife to prove that you love me. Besides, I'm a little curious as to why you're saying all of this tonight. I mean, we've been together for nearly two years and you've never mentioned marriage before."

Stone stroked my hair and stared deeper into my eyes. When he replied it was as if he was trying to reach the epicenter of my soul. "Baby, just because a nigga ain't ever brought it up don't mean it hasn't been on my mind. Real talk, I've been thinking about it for a while now. You're my everything so I want the whole world to know that we belong to each other."

"Stone, are you one hundred percent positive that this is where you want to be? You know I'm not perfect and at times I can be an emotional wreck. Baby, are you sure I'm the one woman you want over all others?"

I needed him to be absolutely sure because if we took the vow *'til death do us part'*, the only way out, seriously, would be by way of the coroner coming to collect the body in a black bag.

"Fuckin' right, I'm sure," he said without hesitation.

My whole face lit up. I scooted closer to him and draped my thigh over his. "So when are you talking about doing this? The baby and getting married," I clarified.

"I'm ready to make my lil' hitta whenever you ready, Ma. As for the wedding, I need to get my money up to buy you a big ass rock. I can't put no little bullshit ring on your finger. Every time the next bitch glance down at your hand, I want her to go home and cuss her nigga out for not blinging her up like I'ma do you, ya heard me."

Puddles of tears welled in my eyes. This was the moment I had been waiting so long for. The promise of commitment was enough for me. I wasn't in any hurry to get a ring. Actions always spoke louder than words. A ring didn't mean shit to me if the man that put it there dogged the fuck out of me.

Plenty of bitches walked around with rings on their fingers daily while their niggas cheated on them behind closed doors. And just because a man claimed to love a woman didn't mean it was true. Quameer and Hollow had both proven that, selling me that *I love you* foolishness and then walking out the door on me without any remorse. I demanded to be the only woman in a man's life, or nothing at all. Stone was talking some heavy shit, but was he worth taking a chance on?

"I feel like I'm ready for that," I said, accepting what I knew I had always desired.

"That's what I wanted to hear," the smile on his face was priceless.

I put my hand under my chin and propped my head up so that I could look down into Stone's eyes as I spoke from the depths of my tortured soul. "I'ma trust you with something those other niggas destroyed, and that's my heart," I said. "Now, you know I've been through hell with niggas and I never planned to love again, but you've managed to break down that wall. It's hard for me to trust completely, but I'm going to do it for you. But Stone, I'm warning you. Don't fuck with my heart."

"What?" He looked offended, but I didn't care. I needed him to understand that I could not endure another heartbreak.

"You heard me," I spoke defiantly. "*Don't—fuck—with—my—heart*," I repeated.

Chapter 9

Quincy and I shared a drink at Santa Fe. The weekday two for one drink special had been our thing on Thursdays for the past year. The tradition of getting together at least once a week had been one we had since high school. It gave us the opportunity to discuss whatever we needed to get off our chest with the unspoken understanding that what was said stayed strictly between us.

It tugged at my conscience to keep some of the things he divulged a secret, but nowhere near as much as my conscience would have felt if I ever betrayed him. Quincy had been the true definition of my big brother and protector since our father vanished from the picture. There was nothing I wouldn't do for him. I was his true ride or die, his Bonnie and he was my Clyde.

Four cups of *Bill Cosby*, Sante Fe's infamous drink, sat on the table in front of us. The drink was guaranteed to knock us on the floor and we were both brave enough to have a pair of cups in front of each one of us. We were discussing Quameer coming at me about money.

"Quameer ain't nothin' but a bitch ass nigga," he said as soon as I'd finished telling him about what happened. "I warned you that dude was foul way back when."

"Nah, I got him," I didn't want my brother to catch a body. In Quincy's eyes, Quameer had already done enough that his funeral should have been years ago, one of the biggest things being when he stole my money.

Craig, my mother's husband, was a sports agent for some top football and basketball players. After marrying my mom, he opened me and Quincy a bank account with twenty-five thousand dollars set to pay out to us when we turned eighteen. For each year that I allowed it to sit untouched, he deposited an additional five thousand until we turned twenty-one. He said that us not touching it demonstrated that we were responsible. Feeling like Quameer was my forever, I told him about the money. That was one of the biggest mistakes of my life.

I was seven months pregnant when he showed up at my momma's door claiming that he had got jacked for his work. "Phat, I need you right now. This nigga gon' body me if I can't make good on what he fronted me."

"How much money do you owe him?" I was terrified that Big Bruiser, the dude that fronted him the work, would make good on his threat. His nickname wasn't given, it was earned.

"Twenty thousand. He gave me until day after tomorrow to make good." He looked like the tears would fall at any moment.

"I don't know where I can get that kind of money from." The thought of my account had never crossed my mind.

"What about that money you told me about? If you give me $30,000 I can get more from him and make the money back plus interest."

"Ok," I agreed without a second thought. This was my son's father, I couldn't raise my baby without him in our lives. "I'll go down to the bank tomorrow."

The next morning I went into the bank and withdrew the money. Needless to say, I never saw a penny of my damn money and when Na'Siah was about a month old he bought a new Dodge Challenger off the lot.

My momma or Craig never found out, but I did mention it to Quincy and Meishelle. They were my confidantes. Quincy wanted his head on a silver platter, but again, I begged on Na'Siah's life. Quameer was a cat with nine lives, because I continually saved him.

"I feel you, but I'm hollering at that nigga tomorrow. Fuck what you sayin'. The only reason he's standing upright is on the strength of my nephew."

"Leave it alone, Quincy," I admonished seriously. "I don't need to give him nothin' to use against me. Beating up Mariah made the judge allow them to keep him longer. And from there things went downhill. One year later and I'm still no closer to getting my baby back. The new lawyer I hired told me to just have a little more patience and not to do anything crazy." I bent my fingers in a quotation sign to emphasis *crazy*.

"I feel you," Quincy sighed, but I could tell that he wanted to get a piece of Quameer's ass. He had put hands on Quameer once when we were younger, but apparently that beating had worn off.

"Just let it play itself out," I advised.

"You never should've fucked with him in the first place. I swear when it comes to men you pick all the wrong ones."

For a second I was taken aback by his harsh criticism because normally Quincy had my back. I figured he was just blowing off steam at the fact that I wouldn't let him step to Quameer with violence. I debated what I should say next. Seeing that he didn't like my choices in men, I wasn't sure if bringing up Stone's proposal was as good an idea as I originally thought. It had really only been a discussion between the two of us and the last thing I needed was him with this bullshit again. Fuck it. We had made a pact not to keep secrets.

And I was anxious to see how he felt about Stone's proposal.

"Nothing much. Stone is talking about getting married and having one of our own."

"You serious right now, Krissett?" He came out of his relaxed position and rubbed his hand over his face.

"Yeah. Why the hell would I be playing about this?" I was offended.

"Come on with the bull, sis. You keep putting your faith in these no good ass niggas. This nigga freshly home from prison and your ass falling for the jail house promises. Open your fucking eyes. I promise you he ain't changed," he stated bluntly.

Now I really wished I had kept my mouth shut because I was getting in my feelings. The only man Quincy thought was right for me was some imaginary ass character out of a comic book. Fuck-ups weren't allowed when it came to me and that shit made him a hypocrite when it came to the subject. Quincy hadn't been to prison, but he had done so much low down and dirty shit behind Meishelle's back that I lost count. He had fucked bitches throughout the city, possibly some in Meishelle's family, and was probably still doing it. I didn't know it to be a fact, but I wouldn't put it past him.

"*You* don't want to go there, do you?" I bucked my eyes and spoke defensively.

"I feel you, sis. Protect yourself first," he warned.

"Yep, now let's talk about you for a minute," I signaled for the barmaid to bring us another round. "Where did the cash come from for Meishelle's ring?"

"What you mean?" He asked as if he didn't know what I was hinting at.

"Don't even try to play me stupid." I knew he made good money as a welder, but he definitely wasn't banking money on that level. Quincy was all about a dollar bill. Although he hadn't dabbled into the game yet, anything else would be open for consideration.

"Sis, I'm good. I had been saving up for a minute to get that ring, real shit."

I raised my brow in suspicion. I knew better than the lie he was trying to sell me. "Real shit, my ass. When you ready, you'll tell me the deal because I know better. All I'll say for now is be careful with whatever it is you're doing."

"I got *me* all day. You know that."

"Exactly, but I hear you. That wrap's on the questions then."

The third drink had started to kick in so it was time to roll. I got a bottle of cold water to drink to sober me up a little before I made my way home. While I sipped and waited we made random conversation about nothing. About fifteen minutes later I felt good enough to get home.

Once outside I stretched my arms out for a hug. My arms couldn't wrap fully around him and my face automatically buried itself into his chest because he was so damn tall.

"You know I always got you, right?" He hated for us to end our evenings on a bad note. I had no doubt he always had my best interest at heart.

"Yeah, yeah." I kidded. "Love you, Quincy."

I broke the embrace and got into my car.

Don't Fu#k With My Heart

Chapter 10

As I pulled into the driveway, I noticed the house lights on. I thought I'd turned them off that morning, but who knew. My ass had been deliriously sleepy the last days since Stone's dick slaying victory. I had been at his job every night since, so I hoped he was off for the evening. Game time had to be restricted to Friday nights only if he was going to act like that.

Opening the door, Na'Siah ran up to me, jumping into my arms.

"Mommy!" He screamed, excited to see me. I embraced him tightly and spun him around. Since I refused to send the money I'd anticipated some drama when it came time to get him this weekend.

He asked me to sit with him at the table as Stone emerged from the kitchen with a plate of his favorite, spaghetti and meat sauce. Walking over, I greeted Stone with a kiss.

"How did you get Na'Siah?"

"Your grams called me. Quameer called her and asked for someone to go pick Na'Siah up from school. He had to leave town."

I shook my head. *That's why that slick bitch needed my fucking money. They better enjoy it now, because it's coming to an end as soon as my baby comes home.* Just to be vindictive I was going after child support. Let that bitch Mariah pay it. That's what she got for allowing a grown ass man to live off her.

Stone told me he picked up tickets for us to go to a basketball game. We only had about two hours so I left them in the dining room and went to pick out some clothes. Na'Siah still hadn't finished eating so I jumped in the tub first. Stone scared the hell out of me coming into the bathroom while I was lotioning my body.

"Damn, baby, I wanna tear that ass up right now," Stone commented the moment he stepped inside. The look said he wanted to devour me right there.

"You know that won't happen right now. I can't take you quietly," I told him as I reached for my robe.

Before he could reply, Na'Siah interrupted, knocking on the door.

"Stone it's my turn," he called out.

"Ok, lil'man. I thought I could sneak in before you."

"No. I saw you."

Putting on my robe, I waved my finger at Stone as if he'd acted out like a bad child. Opening the door, Na'Siah stepped into the bathroom.

"Let's go get your things, Na'Siah." I said, picking him up.

"I'll take care of you later, big baby," I said, winking at Stone.

"You promise?" he asked.

"Pinky swear," I answered and we locked fingers, sealing the agreement.

"When we get back I got something I want to run past you," he called out after me.

"Ok, boo." I replied.

Na'Siah wiggled and squirmed to get out of my arms once we were at his room door. He recognized that each time he'd come over he'd have something new. The remote control fire truck on the bed was this weekend's treat. His mouth dropped open as he checked out the truck. He ran out of the room for Stone to open it. I cherished how easy he was to please.

Gathering his underclothes for his bath, I went to the bathroom and ran some water. Adding a small amount of Scooby Doo bubble bath, I called out for Na'Siah to come get in the tub.

Once he'd reached the tub, I took his clothes off and put him inside the water. He giggled, playing around with the bubbles, blowing them in the air. He even put some in his hair and gave me some to play with. He stopped as if something suddenly came to his mind.

"Mommy, what's a bitch?"

"Where did you hear that?" I was taken aback by the question.

"Daddy and Mariah always say it about you."

Rage filled me. I already knew they talked about me, but these two low down bitches did it in front of my baby? Na'Siah wasn't stupid, so they knew exactly what they were doing. I shook my head as I held back the urge to call and serve both their ugly asses an ear full. That was the reason they didn't need custody, they were too immature to handle it.

My weekends with my son excluded any mention of them, under no circumstances did I question Na'Siah about what they did together. The most I'd ask was how his day went. I was determined to be the bigger woman, though. They probably wanted me to say something because they both planned to interrogate him as soon as he got home.

"Sometimes, adults say things that they don't mean," I faked a smile.

"Then, why do they say them?"

"Because they're angry or upset about something. Daddy doesn't hate Mommy, or we wouldn't have had you, alright?"

"Okay," he held out his hands. "I'm wrinkled now."

"So let's get you all washed up."

I used the rest of the time to boggle him down with questions about his day such as what he learned, had for lunch, and about his homework. This was my first time having him during the week since he started Pre-K. I was somewhat disappointed to find out that Stone had helped him with his homework because I really wanted to help. The school never sent it home on Fridays due to it being the weekend.

I turned the TV on Scooby Doo after I dressed him and then went to get myself together. It fascinated me how much he loved the old school cartoon. It was the only cartoon I'd hang up all hours of the night watching when I was pregnant with him.

I played in the mirror with my hair to see how I wanted to wear it. I had finished up with a high ponytail before I slipped into my 7 For All Mankind jeans, matching Pelicans shirt, and Kevin Durant high top tennis shos. I wasn't a huge fan of makeup unless it was a special occasion, but my red lipstick spoke volumes across my plump lips. I wore that religiously. I onced over myself in the mirror, giving my final look the stamp of approval.

Stone wasn't ready yet when I knocked on the door so me and Na'Siah moved to the living room to watch TV. I dozed off while we waited.

Stone tapping me on the shoulder woke me up. "You ready?"

"Yeah," I yawned.

"Do you wanna stay in? I can take him and let you get some rest," he offered.

Stone was so considerate. I thought that quality was impossible to find in men based on my previous relationships. Especially since they had been so selfish and all about themselves, fuck what I felt about anything.

"No, I'm okay. I wouldn't miss this night with my two favorite men for the world," I placed a kiss on the top of Na'Siah's head.

"You ready?" I asked Na'Siah.

"I sure am. What's the surprise mommy?" He hollered.

We were still working on the difference between inside and outside voices. I'd let him slide though, because I could barely compose myself.

Turning off the TV, lights, and setting the alarm, I locked the door. We took Stone's Escalade since Na'Siah's car seat was already in it. Fastening him in, he wiggled in excitement as we backed out of the garage and headed to the game.

Na'Siah eyes grew wild when we'd arrived at the Smoothie King Center. The three leveled, green, iridescent tiled arena contained a huge projector screen on the left side. The building itself could've easily been overlooked with no problem since it sat directly behind the enormous Mercedes Benz Superdome.

Getting to our seats, Stone took Na'Siah and left me to watch the beginning of the game alone. They came back with hot dogs, nachos, popcorn, and pasta bags from the arena store. I could see he had spent over a hundred dollars buying jerseys and whatever else it was Na'Siah had picked up.

"Look what else we picked out," he had all-into-one's and a baby's jersey.

"Mommy, that's for little brother or sister, Stone said," Na'Siah chimed in.

These two together needed restraint. "I should have gone as the chaperon," I said with a chuckle, taking my pasta from Stone's hand.

"It's what he wanted," Stone passed the blame like a guilty child.

"So you're not in control?" I twisted up my lips.

"Nope," he responded. The way he was with Na'Siah exhibited what a great father he would be with his own seed.

***

Stone lay relaxed hands behind his head while in the bed watching TV. The four wall speakers were blasting the Sport's Center report. I loved seeing my man crush, Ray Lewis, in a suit. Stone's jealousy showed quite a bit every time I bit my lip in reaction to seeing him.

Crossing over to my side of the bed, I fluffed my pillows behind my back. The ideal conversation would have been more about the marriage and family situation, maybe setting a date. Although I could mask the shit out of it, insecurities still existed since his release and I needed constant reassurance that a committed relationship with me was what he *really* wanted.

"So what you wanna talk about?"

"I've been thinking that I wanna try some new things in our sex life," Stone eluded.

I wasn't sure where he was going because I questioned what it was we hadn't done sexually. He got pussy and ass in every imaginable position there could be. I bought costumes, a book of positions, and even toys to make sure we kept it lively.

"Such as?" I raised a brow with piqued curiosity.

"I wanna do a threesome."

"Come again." My ears had to be playing with me. This nigga had to be out his damn mind. I already needed convincing that he wanted to be with me, his request could do some serious damage to my self-esteem. He could have saved that money on those game tickets if that was why he got them.

"I want to do a threesome," he reiterated without batting an eye.

I sat speechless. There I was thinking I was putting my shit down right, making this nigga never fathom being with another woman, and he had the nerve to ask me to allow another bitch into my bedroom. I was about two seconds from putting his ass out of my bed *and* my damn house, for good!

"Where the fuck you see stupid written on my face, Stone?" I seethed.

"Where the hell you get that out of what I asked?"

"You just committed a few damn months ago, just to me after fucking over me with a slew of bitches. So that's the only way I can see you coming at me like this," I replied, clueless as to how he could think a threesome would ever be ok.

"Listen, baby girl, them hos in the street didn't mean shit to me so neither did the experience. I wanted to share this with you."

"Share this with me," I laughed. "Stone this is about you. I don't do pussy, only dick. And my lone pussy must not be doing shit for you."

"It ain't that, Ma. You makin' more out this shit than what it has to be."

"Why, because I didn't just say yes?"

"Nah, because this ain't about another bitch, this is about us."

I heard Quincy's words play in my head, *jail house talk.* That was exactly what this nigga was pulling right now. I quietly got up and out of the bed. Putting on my slippers and robe, I walked out of the bedroom door.

"Krissett," he called out just above a whisper while reaching for my wrist.

I yanked my wrist back before he could grab it and stomped down the hallway until I had reached Na'Siah's room.

"Krissett? Ma, come back in here," he continued to call down the hallway.

I had no words for him. I didn't know what kind of bitch Stone was taking me for, but I wasn't her. I marched down the hallway to Na'Siah's room, he'd just given me an excuse to spend more time with my little man.

The clock on his nightstand read two in the morning and the sandman still hadn't come my way. My mind had remained focused on the threesome proposition Stone had made, the idea that he was doing this for us was inconceivable. I had never considered adding another bitch to my bed, females weren't my get down and never would be. I worried too much about him fucking with another female than adding one to our equation willingly. It was all about what he wanted with his selfish ass.

A few hours ago I had given him credit for being considerate, but it was nothing but an underlying motive. *When would I be adequate enough? When would a man come along that was willing to give all I was giving for them?*

Chapter 11

I eased out of the bed. Na'Siah had begun to squirm from my tightened grip on him. In the living room I tossed a Lithium in my mouth followed by a shot of Crown to chase it. The liquor helped amp the effect of the pill since they no longer worked on their own. Restless, I couldn't bring myself to get back into the bed with Na'Siah and rejoining Stone wasn't up for consideration.

I decided to watch my favorite show, Criminal Minds, since it was on when I channel surfed. After about three episodes, the TV began to watch me. I was disturbed out of my slumber when Stone came into the living room shaking me at the shoulder.

"Shit!" I hollered as I scrambled to my feet. He startled me.

"Ooh, mommy said a bad word," Na'Siah said, sitting at the kitchen table. He was fully dressed, swinging his feet from the chair, eating cereal.

"I got him," Stone offered. "I'll take him to school on my way to work. Just make sure you're on time for work."

With no response to Stone, I walked over to Na'Siah and kissed him on the cheek. "Have a great day. I'll see you this evening for dinner, baby."

"Krissett, we need to discuss that issue from last night," Stone suggested.

"Later," I sharply spoke as I closed the bedroom door behind me.

Thank goodness it was Friday so I could dress down a little. I turned on the news for the morning traffic update, but instead ended up hearing about overnight killings and the ongoing search for a suspect in a bank robbery a few months ago. I sent a quick text to Meishelle that we needed to get together for a girls talk.

Outside, the sun shined like a flashlight being held directly in my face. Reaching the last step, I noticed that Stone's slick ass had left his truck in a clear attempt to get some conversation out of me. He knew we would have to meet up and exchange vehicles so he could go to work that night, but I would show him.

My aggravation subsided when my phone rang while I sat in the morning rush traffic. "How may I help you?" I answered enthusiastically, noticing it was Meishelle.

"Don't even play with me after you texted that you needed to talk," Meishelle chuckled.

"I'm pretty sure I said later and not now."

"Excuse me, Ms. Baptiste. You'll take the time I give you. What's going on, chick?"

I told her that the conversation I wanted to have was more of one in person over some drinks. She said that we could have dinner after we finished running for the weekend. She had plans to select the dresses that we would wear for the wedding. She wanted to pick something that would cater to everyone's shape.

"That it includes Janasia, too," she added, trying to sneak that little detail by me.

I didn't know how to respond. I looked up just in time to slam on brakes and avoid running into the car stopped at the red light.

"Come again," I said.

"Before you go in, you already know I didn't want to," she tried to ease it over. "It kind of involved a family intervention from my momma and my grandmother."

"Well, it doesn't leave you much time to find another maid of honor. You already know how I feel about that bitch, and I'm not about to be in her presence."

"Come on, Krissett. You know I need you there with me. This is the biggest day of my life," she pleaded.

"You can save that shit," I gestured with my hand although she couldn't see me. "That bitch did the unthinkable. You can play along on your wedding day to satisfy your family, but I'm sure in the fuck not about to."

"Krissett, are you serious right now?" she asked incredulously.

She was trying to pull on my emotions, but the hell with all that. I stood firm on not doing the fake bullshit. This was about my principles and only the Almighty could change those. Feeling myself getting upset, I pulled into a parking lot near the job.

When Na'siah was about six months, Quameer vanished into thin air. At least a week went by with no calls or texts before I got the police involved. His mother claimed she had no idea, but the police magically jogged her memory. They found him in good health at his new girlfriend Janasia's house.

Janasia was Meishelle's youngest aunt and Na'Siah's godmother. We had been friends since my mid-teenage years. My momma didn't care for her much because she was at least sixteen years older than us. She felt that a woman that old had no business hanging with kids, it demonstrated how childish she could be. To me she was the best. She allowed me and Quameer to cut school at her house, we spent nights together and just about anything went. I had no idea she was capable of such horrific disloyalty.

"Serious as life itself. That bitch was supposed to have been my friend and instead she'd turned out to be treacherous," I said, getting angrier by the minute.

"And after her actions were exposed I beat her ass right along with you. I put your friendship before my family and this is how you repay me," Meishelle said becoming choked up.

"Family or not, you beat her ass because what she did crossed all boundaries," I shouted.

"I can't believe you backing me into a corner like this, Krissett."

"You asking me to take ten steps back into the past so you can step into the future? What the fuck do you want from me?" I screamed. This time louder.

"I'm asking you to face your past and accept it for what it is, sacrifice like I have done for you all these years. You've moved past Quameer and I want you to move past her," she sniffled.

I couldn't believe she insinuated I was some fair-weather ass friend that was all about self. She hadn't experienced true heartache so she wouldn't understand the next to impossible act of forgiving those who hurt you beyond repair. Before she and Quincy hooked up she'd had a few high school relationships, but nothing serious because her mother didn't play the boyfriend game. I had to be her alibi just to go out with a guy. She would have to tell her mother we were going to a respectable place and then meet him there.

In my mind, Quameer did what any nigga would do when staring pussy in the face because it has no name. This trifling bitch had taken a vow in church to care for my baby if something happened to me while she was actually the one plowing a knife in my back. Then after Quameer left she had the audacity to call and ask if she could get Na'Siah on the weekends. Even Quameer's dumb ass had the decency to disappear altogether.

"I *tolerate* Quameer because a judge ordered me too. Big difference," I went silent.

"But—" she started to interrupt.

"But what?" I interjected.

"At some point you have to forgive her to move on with your own life. Right now that bitch is still winning. You're going to be miserable on my wedding day while this ho smiling."

I completely lost it. The tears that streamed down my face were hot. "What the fuck you mean *forgive* her, Meishelle?" I pounded my fist on the dashboard. *Forgive* her because I allowed her to cry on my shoulder about having chlamydia, but she didn't tell me that I needed to be checked too because she was fucking me man?"

"Yes, that's exactly what I'm saying. It's time you be honest with yourself. You making that lame ass excuse of forgiveness for Quameer, but regardless of how it happened, she didn't make him fuck her."

"I'll let God *forgive* her for her sins because I will show no mercy," I replied defiantly. "You know I love you and my brother with everything in me, but the wedding is out. I'll make no apology."

"You never have to be sorry for exposing who you are," she finalized the conversation and disconnected the call.

I pulled down the visor and checked my appearance. My eyes were bloodshot red. Glancing up, I dreaded the high rise building before me. There was not a fiber in my body that wanted to go to work, but there was no sense in fighting it. Everything couldn't start falling apart like this.

Nothing personal, it was business, I told myself as I proceeded out of the parking lot to work.

Don't Fu#k With My Heart

Chapter 12

The weekend had been nonstop foolishness. For some odd reason Stone believed I hadn't heard his full point of view regarding the ménage a trois, so he tried to present it Saturday and again on Sunday. It enraged me each time, causing me to spend time away from home.

Between Quincy, my momma, and Hattie Mae I received no less than seventy-five text messages about my decision to leave the wedding party. I responded to each with a simple *okay,* so they'd know I was alright. I wasn't trying to debate them about my decision. Even Mrs. Williams, Meishelle's mother, had sent me a message asking me to call her. With no peace on the home or family front I was in desperate need to get away.

Bright and early Monday morning, I headed to the Louis Armstrong International Airport for my flight to the 'A'. I needed to getaway to think for a while. I made it to the airport on time for my nine-thirty morning flight. Once I boarded the plane, settled into my seat, and checked my phone before takeoff, I saw that Stone had texted me.

8:20 a.m.: How long will you be gone for Ma?

9:10 a.m.: I'm not sure Stone. Maybe a week.

9:13 a.m.: Shit don't make no sense. If you would just listen.

9:20 a.m.: I don't need to hear a damn thing about it and don't you dare think about bringing another bitch in my house. You seem to let your dick lead your decisions.

The flight attendant advised that for now phones had to be powered off. My mind wandered to whether or not Stone would really bring another bitch on my turf. History tended to repeat itself and Stone had a long and extensive one.

Takeisha, a.k.a Keedy, and the condom incident had been only one of a million.

There was no one to call to check on Stone and the house and the last thing I needed was for them to know I was having doubts about Stone's loyalty. That was the bullshit even more so that I needed to take my mind off. When drinks were offered I used mine to pop two Lithium to calm my nerves. *You don't have proof he has done anything else I exhaled.*

'Love Knows No Boundaries' by Coffee served as my in-flight entertainment. I was so engrossed in it that time passed within the blink of an eye. I texted my cousin, Schtanya, to let her know I had touched down. She told me she had to pick up her kids and that we could catch up tomorrow night for dinner. Stone had replied to my last message, but I deleted it. *All about me* were the words that resonated in my head.

Seeking consolation at Lenox Square Mall, I heard a male voice calling my name. My mind had to be playing tricks on me because I hadn't given my real name to a man in over four years.

"Krissett," I heard again as the person came up behind me.

Never in a million years did I think I would cross paths with him again. My eyes widened to grasp who he was.

"Damn, Phat, you look good. It's been a long time, but your face hasn't changed," Hollow, my low down ex, eyed me up and down. He had been my first love and heartache. Our situation kicked off my downward spiral which started during middle school.

The years had been good to him I had to admit. He stood six feet, two inches, chocolate brown skin with a nice fade, slim with tattoos decorating his forearms. His smile was perfectly aligned, he should have been a model for Colgate.

"Hi, Hollow. How've you been?" I kept it simple. I wanted to run as far away from him as possible, but Quincy's words played in my mind. *Never let 'em know they fazed you.*

"I'm good, can't complain about shit. What you doing out here?"

"Came to get away for a minute. You?" I was trying to be polite, but I was far from interested in what he actually had to say.

He told me that he had moved to Atlanta with his girl who had gotten on with the government. He went home one night to his bags packed and another female sitting on the sofa. She told him that she no longer wanted to be with him. He was actually trying to relocate back to New Orleans, Karma was definitely a bitch.

Me and Hollow had been together about four months when he asked me to cut school. I sat next to him in his friend's bedroom in Hollygrove, an area in Uptown New Orleans, not far from my school. The room was the size of a match box. There was a small twenty inch TV on a wooden TV stand and a mattress and box spring on a frame. The window curtain was a sheet and there were no closet doors. I kept looking around the room like a paranoid kid.

He hit me with the mental games about being special in his life and wanting to be my first. "You know I love you, right?" Those three words, eight letters that have only one meaning, meant the world to me coming from him. Hollow was the sun, moon, and stars on my earth.

"I love you, too, Hollow."

I succumbed to the pressure. Girls had always tried to come at him, so whatever I needed to do to keep him was what I would do.

"Okay. Take off your clothes and lay on your back. I'll do everything else."

I followed his instructions and he stripped down to his boxers, rejoining me in the bed.

He started kissing me, sucking my neck, breasts, nipples, spreading my legs and climbing between them. He rubbed the tip of his dick in my split. It felt so good. A minute later the pleasure ended and the pain started. I felt a poke, but it was hitting a wall. He pushed deeper and deeper. The more he pushed, the more it hurt.

"Hollow, it hurts," I whined.

"I'm almost in."

"Please, stop," I pleaded.

"Shut the fuck up. Remember you said you loved me, and if you do you will do this."

He rammed his dick into me as hard as he could. I tried to scream from the pain but nothing came out. Something cold and wet ran down my leg. He bit into my breasts as hard as he could and pinned my hands so I couldn't move. Pain and burning sensations shot up through my stomach and into my chest. I closed my eyes tightly, wishing he would hurry up and finish. Finally, I heard him grunt and he rolled off of me.

Getting up and gathering my clothes, I saw that the sheets were stained with blood. It had soaked completely through them and into the mattress. Hollow lay on the opposite side refusing to look at me. Flames scorched the juncture between my weak, wobbly legs.

"Can you bring me back to school, please? I'm bleeding."

"Nah, You'll have to catch the bus. Just plug yourself up until you can get home"

My brain instantly went on mute. I picked up my clothes and ran across the hallway. I wiped off as much blood as I could and then stuffed a whole bunch of toilet paper inside my vagina. Returning to the room for my book bag, Hollow had gotten up and put on his boxers.

He opened the room door and handed me a garbage bag that held the stripped bed linens.

"Throw this on the sidewalk on your way out," he passed me the bag.

I couldn't do anything but walk off.

Two weeks later, he called to apologize saying he didn't know what had gotten into him. His motive was only more sex, which came out when he asked three days later. When my breasts burned, there weren't enough hours in the day for sleep, and I couldn't keep anything down, he disappeared all over again.

"So how long you here for?"

"Just until Thursday."

"I feel you," he bobbed his head at my answer. "Well, you think I can get one of those nights with you?"

"No. I have a man and I don't think he would be too happy about me having dinner with an ex." I replied. I had enough shit going on without running into his motherfucking ass as it was. I had been told when it rains it pours, right then, between issues with Stone and Meishelle and running into Hollow it began to feel like a downpour.

"We would be just two old friends having a meal. What's the problem with that?"

"Umm, I can't say that I consider you a friend. Friends don't treat friends the way you treated me." I was reaching my limit with being pleasant. In no way could that dude be serious. True, me and Stone were beefing, but I wasn't about to step out with anyone, especially not Hollow. I loved my man too much, he would never be worth me losing Stone

"I tried to call you and apologize but you wouldn't take my calls. How about you take my number and hit me up if you change your mind?"

"What would your apology have changed? You can't give me my baby back, Hollow. You turned your back on me when I needed you the most, so thanks but no thanks. I have to go."

I turned around and walked off. I had been through a lot of shit since then, but nothing comparable to what Hollow had done me. He had robbed me of my innocence, my virginity, and partially my baby girl. It took me years to learn how to cope with all the hurt he inflicted. I had moved on to the future and Hollow was a part of a past I never, *ever*, wanted to relive.

Chapter 13

Schtanya wanted me try this new place she claimed had soul food like New Orleans. We arrived at Beautiful Restaurant on Casade Road SW. They were known to have some of the best food in Atlanta. I was hoping they did because the closet I had come that far was Gladys Knight Chicken and Waffles and I hated to risk it for nasty food.

It was a small, dimly lit building that sat on the corner. There were only a few tables and chairs, so they could never have a huge crowd to dine in. Beautiful resembled Two Sisters on Bienville Street back home, except it had a cafeteria, buffet style set up. Seeing all the different selections to choose from made my mouth water.

Macaroni and cheese, collard greens, cabbage, candied yams, baby ribs, cornbread, lemon cake, and more. It was a good thing I had gotten my work out on in the hotel because I was going all in. I ordered the steak with double mac and cheese, cabbage, cornbread and banana pudding. The lemon cake with icing I would take back to the room.

"So what's been up?" She asked as we took our seats.

"Girl, nothing much. Just wanted to get away and relax for a minute."

"Krissett, please, we are family, I know better than that. So you going to let me help or you want to allow it to bother you more?" She obviously didn't believe me.

Since Meishelle wasn't speaking to me and Schtanya was the next closet to a best friend, I divulged Stone's proposition.

"Me and Bryan had one or two before we were married. Since the kids we haven't had a chance, but if we do, I'm game," she replied casually.

111

"What?" I almost choked on my first bite, completely dumbfounded. "You and Bryan seem some wholesome."

My vision for Schtanya and her man was the missionary position only. She was the only woman I knew who had obtained the American Dream, a career as an attorney, successful doctor for a husband, two story home with the backyard, two point five kids, *and* the dog. To my knowledge she had all the happiness and peace she desired without needing help from another woman.

"Wholesome?" She laughed at my response. "I keep my man happy by any means necessary. Side bitches have become the new trend."

She had definitely intrigued me. My mind raced with questions. It baffled me how she could be comfortable allowing another woman in her bed with the worry of her man going anywhere.

Her first reason was that it was what every man fantasized about. She felt that with an open relationship she had to actually worry less about Bryan stepping out on her. He had no reason to look elsewhere if all his needs were fulfilled at home. She felt that if Bryan wanted to leave he would do so anyway, regardless of her inviting the woman into their home. No relationship was guaranteed whether she let another female in or not. If it was meant to be he could meet the same female on the street and leave her all the same.

Plus, she enjoyed the women as much as him. In her opinion there was nothing like a woman's tongue. Two women knew what it took to please each other. The touch of her hands, softness of her body, the intimacy of it was cosmic according to her. After hearing her explicit description I was ready to find a bitch on the street and try her out. Between my thighs was becoming most. What went on in the "A" stayed in the "A".

"I'm not sure if I can trust Stone like that just yet?" Men in my past had played some extremely fire acting roles when it came to caring for me. They could have won Oscars for their outstanding skills.

"I can't tell you how to handle the situation honey, but you really need to ask yourself why you are with him. Make your decision with no regrets." She changed the subject. "So what did you get at the mall yesterday?"

"Nothing out of the ordinary, except a dinner invite from Hollow?" I replied cynically.

"I know you turned his ass down, right?" She crumpled her nose up.

"You know better than to ask that question." I would not even dignify that question with a response. What was under-stood didn't need to be stated.

"Occasionally you do slip up, so I just needed to verify."

She said she would come down in another two weeks or so to be fitted for her bridesmaid's gown. She was also in Meishelle and Quincy's wedding. I broke the news to her that I would wasn't in the wedding party any longer since Janasia had been added. Being an attorney, she handled most situations like she was in a court of law. She would listen to both sides and then argue the case from the perspective of the person not present, but the final verdict was always left for you to make. I loved that quality about my cousin.

Don't Fu#k With My Heart

Chapter 14

Every morning, I found an mp3 message in my inbox from Stone. The subject line read "How I feel about you" with a song attached. Brian McKnight "Do I Ever Cross Your Mind" was one of my favorites. I limited my reply to a simple good morning and thanked him for the song. It warmed my heart to think that he missed me, but my mind always ruined the moment with thoughts of what-ifs.

The rest of the week was so refreshing, Schtanya and I did something every day to keep my mind occupied. For me the highlight was a wine tasting in downtown Atlanta. I made note of which ones I would add to my collection when I returned home. Stone also paged me daily

On my last night I'd ended up cancelling my usual plan of dinner with her. Instead, I settled in with a bottle of Patron. This trip had been nothing I'd expected, but I couldn't leave without the answers I'd come for.

The first situation was Meishelle and the wedding. I wanted to do what I felt might be the easiest so that the liquor would have time to kick in. I had to admit, a lot of what she said in our argument made sense. She *had* sacrificed a lot for me. Since we were thirteen there was not a time that I woke up in the hospital and she wasn't there. When I realized the possibility that I might have been pregnant, she went with me to confirm my suspicions.

One Saturday morning we pretended we were going to catch the bus to the movies, but instead went to Planned Parenthood. When the test came back positive I trembled in fear. I couldn't tell my momma and grandmother the truth. But I couldn't hide it forever. By the time I was three months it became obvious that something was up.

When I lost my baby girl, she was right there by my bed-side, apologizing.

We had made our weekday round through the game room and stopped at McDonald's to eat. When we were done, we split up to catch our individual buses at the Krauss building on Canal and Basin Street. I was fourteen years old and five months pregnant. My stomach was noticeable if someone focused hard enough. My shape came early like my menstrual cycle. By thirteen my bra size had exceeded my mom and I had a nice butt. At that point my baby girl was giving me the hips to make my coke bottle size complete.

Hollow hadn't taken the news too good, being nineteen at the time, but was warming up to the idea. He was nervous about my parents finding out and pressing charges. That's what he got for thinking with his dick. Men always paid attention to the shape of females instead of the more relevant age. Hattie Mae eventually calmed my mother down, telling her that what was done was done, so there was really nothing that would come out of him going to jail.

We were a little later than normal so the usual crowd had subsided. As I waited for the St. Bernard bus to come, I heard a voice say, "That's the bitch right there."

Five older girls began heading in my direction. Me and Meishelle kept to ourselves so I had no reason to believe they were talking about me.

Surrounding me, one stepped in my face and said, "Bitch, I heard you fuckin' with my man?"

"Your man?" I questioned, confused.

To my knowledge Hollow lived with his sister and aunt. He said his sister tripped about him using the house phone so we always talked before she came home.

"Yeah, bitch? Hollow is my man. We have two babies together. Where do you think he stays?" She bucked.

"He told me you were his sister. I didn't know he had a girl."

This shit was starting to really piss me off. Normally I would have bucked back instantly, but being pregnant I was in no shape to fight. But I couldn't wait to get his ass on the phone.

She eyed me intensely, head to toe, while the others just stood around being cheerleaders for everything she said.

"Wait, hold the fuck up. You pregnant?" She hollered out.

I stood there for a minute, debating on how to answer. I was clearly outnumbered, but before I could open my mouth to answer, the ho swung on me. Before I had the chance to swing back the other four bitches were pounding on me too.

My ability to swing was limited with the heavy book sack on my back. I didn't see it going down like that so I never dropped it. I hovered to protect myself from the blows, but someone pulled me to the ground by my hair. Focusing on my baby, I tried to protect my stomach as they kicked me in my face, arms, and legs. My eyes wouldn't open and I tasted the blood that came from my nose. I screamed for them to stop, but a kick to my mouth silenced me. My shoulders, arms, and hands throbbed from the constant lashing my body was taking. I wasn't sure how much longer I could take it. My limbs began to fall limp as the pain turned to numbness.

I heard someone screaming, "Call the police! Call the police! You girls stop it!"

The blows lessened as people began pulling them off of me.

"Krissett!" I heard Meishelle scream as I felt a glob of spit hit me in the face.

"You slut!" Hollow's girl spit in my face, simultaneously kicking me in my belly.

"AHHH!" I winced from the excruciating pain that exuded from the pit of my stomach right before I blacked out.

When I came to at the hospital they told me they couldn't locate a heartbeat and I would be induced so I could pass the baby. We held a small memorial service and I named her Ketoyia. I stayed three additional days until I was deemed stabilized.

My eyes were swollen shut and my shoulder dislocated along with extensive bruising of my face and arms. I assumed it was a relief off Hollow's back when I lost our baby because not once did he set foot into my hospital room or so much as call me to see how I was doing.

When Mrs. Williams found out why I was in the hospital, she forbade Meishelle to be my friend. She said I was a bad influence on her. It didn't stop her, though. She took multiple punishments and ass whippings to remain my girl.

As we got older she slept on my sofa to make sure I didn't hurt myself on nights that seemed rough for me. She had probably thrown more punches and kicks when we got in the fights about Quameer with other females. I owed her that much. Besides, that bitch Janasia, knowing she was the reason I didn't come to the wedding would only give her life. I wanted nothing but a slow, miserable death for her ass.

Those were just a few examples of the selflessness Meishelle had displayed. So if my bestie wanted to me stand beside Janasia to be by her side on her wedding day, I was more than willing.

Last but not least was Stone. I set the expectation of being open and honest in the relationship, so I set the stage for this conversation to be introduced.

It wasn't as simple as Schtanya made it to be in my case with Stone and his track record. A situation like that could be hazardous and toxic for my relationship and if Stone left I could only blame myself. Shit, I would have partially given him away to the next bitch if I went along with his idea. I went above and beyond in the bedroom to make him happy. There wasn't anything I wouldn't do as long as it remained between me and him.

From the beginning, he had stepped up financially and somewhat emotionally. He'd taken over the responsibility of paying my bills from my mom and Quincy to ensure I went to school. Semesters when I had huge gaps in between classes, he picked me up for lunch. He made sure I attended all my psychologist appointments and adhered to my medications. When it came to Na'Siah, Stone was his father in my eyes. Na'Siah had actually thought he was before Quameer brought his no good ass into the picture. It took a few months for us to break his habit of calling Stone daddy.

Up to that point, outside of his bedroom proposal I still had no reasons to doubt him. He answered when I called, texted throughout the day to check on me, and was very attentive. I decided to exercise some confidence in my ability to make decisions and the bond me and Stone shared. I would give him the threesome, but not without an understanding and rules. Strict rules.

Don't Fu#k With My Heart

Chapter 15

On my way home from the airport I decided to get in some final alone time before I picked up Na'Siah for the weekend. I made my way to the lake off of West End Blvd. My momma texted, letting me know she wanted to keep Na'Siah so she could bring him to a party over the weekend. I told her I wanted to have dinner with him, but would bring him after his bath.

The clear skies and light breeze made it such an ideal day. Like a kindergartener, I sat Indian style on the concrete bank and became mesmerized by the calmness of the water. Water was a lot like life. Storms came, creating rough spurts, but when it was over the water returned to a calm state. I could definitely enjoy life like this. I had gotten lost in random thoughts, but the orange hue of the sky as the sun began to set meant I overstayed and it was time to go home.

On the way I called Hattie Mae. She had been trying to get in touch with me since before I left for Atlanta.

"Hey, Sugar. Where you been?" She caught me off guard by being calm.

"I went by Schtanya's for a few days to get my head clear." She told me Quincy and Meishelle had been over about me leaving the wedding party. Before she could do her speech, pointing out everything they had ever done for me in life, I told her that I had decided to remain in the wedding party. I hesitated before continuing, "Hollow asked about you."

"Oh, yeah? How is he doing?"

"He seemed to be ok. He invited me to dinner, but I declined."

"You're still mad at him after all these years, huh?

"Of course," I replied. I had no reason not to be.

"You shouldn't be, because it means you haven't really moved on," she preached. "Otherwise seeing him would not bother you at all. I know he hurt your heart a whole lot. When you lost the baby everything spun out of control, but guilt is what kept him away."

"I have moved on. I am with Stone now." It was very few times when I saw things differently than Hattie Mae, but this was one.

"You have to forgive him. Hurt builds up and you'll end up taking it out on Stone. That's not fair to him. He's a good man and deserves a fair shot."

"You're right. I'll work on it."

"Alright, sweetheart." We ended the call.

* * *

Pulling into the garage, I ignored Stone's truck parked in the driveway. Checking my car clock, I saw that it was the end of the day. *He must have started the carpool they were discussing,* I thought.

The sight of rose petals draping the carpet from the door to the bathroom halted my footsteps inside of my home. Lit candles illuminated the dining room table set for two. The light sounds of Freddie Jackson bellowed through the speakers mounted in each corner of the room.

"There's something that I want to say, but words sometimes get in the way... You are my lady. You're ev'rything I need and more. You are my lady..."

Stone emerged from the bedroom in a crisp, white tee that accentuated his broad shoulders and a pair of jeans hung off of his chiseled waistline perfectly. The newest pair of Jordans adorned his feet, highlighting his thuggish style. His dreads were freshly twisted and hung to his shoulders. The smell of his Clive Christian cologne penetrated my nostrils and immediately caused a light mist to form in my panties.

"Hey, love," he continued his walk down the hallway toward me.

"Hi," was my only response.

"What's up with you? You been dodging me, huh?" He stood before me.

"Nah, I'm cool. Just needed time to think about what you brought to the table." I pronounced my words slowly to indicate that I was slightly confused about what was going on.

He had invited me to the table for a dinner of steaks with smothered onions, fully loaded mashed potatoes along with sautéed kale. Have a seat." He gestured to the table with his hands.

A few minutes later, the aroma of the food signified its arrival. Starting the conversation off he said, "If I thought my proposition would have pissed you off so much I would have just left it alone. You said if I ever wanted anything you would rather me ask you than go out in the streets and ask another broad to do it."

"That's true," I sampled my dinner. "While in Atlanta, I realized if you were to leave me after I did a threesome you were never truly here to begin with."

"Krissett, a nigga not going anywhere after all this time," he interrupted me. "I want you in my life permanently. I'm ready to add another baby to our unit. No one can make me walk away from that. I'm trying to make this official."

"I understand. My answer is going to be yes, but I do feel like we need to set some rules to this so you don't get shit twisted."

His eyes showed the excitement he was trying to contain.

"It can't be any bitch off of the street, absolutely no one from your past. She has to be recently tested, she and I will have to be compatible, and we both have to agree on her." I raised a finger on my right hand for each stipulation. "My preference is that she's a lesbian so she doesn't chase *my* dick. But don't look for this to happen overnight.

"Damn. You really thought this shit out. But, I respect everything you put out there. I'll let you find the woman, then."

I allowed the selection of the female to be up to him because it was his idea and I had no clue where to begin. Once he found her I would step in and there was to be no contact between them until the night of the threesome. He had a female cousin that got down with chicks he wanted to holla at about some possible. I just reiterated not fucking up the trust that I was placing in him.

"I got you, that's my word," he promised. "So enough talking about how much I love you, are you ready for me to show you?" He placed his hand between my legs.

"How are you going to do that?" I responded.

He grabbed my hand and guided me to the kitchen. He took his time unbuttoning each item of clothing I wore, allowing it to hit the floor. I struggled to contain the moistness forming in my cave.

"Wait right here," he summoned me.

"Sure, baby," I hissed.

Positioning me on the kitchen island, he placed a blindfold over my eyes.

I heard the doors to the refrigerator and freezer open before he returned. He directed me to sip the contents of the glass he placed at my lips. The taste of my favorite Butterfly Moscato pleased my palate.

"Taste this," he requested tracing my lips with pieces of fresh, succulent fruit, presenting it with a passionate exchange through our mouths.

"Mmm," I savored the sweet juices of fruit as some dripped from my mouth. The sensuality of the moment drove me wild.

"Now open your mouth wide," was his second order.

I complied and he glided a piece of ice in and out of my mouth. He slid it down my neck and chest, tracing each nipple before it melted under the scorch of my skin. My nipples became erect at the touch of the ice and condensation began building. My senses further soared as he began sucking on my neck. Continuing to feed me ice, he easily floated it over my warming flesh and he traced it with his tongue. The warming and cooling of my flesh sent multiple tremors down my spine.

His tongue caressed my skin, retreating into the love cave below my waist that awaited him. Instantly at the touch my knees buckled. He quickly secured me in his hold, reflexively elevating me to the edge of the island.

"Oh shit, baby. Eat your dessert." I grabbed his head with both of my hand, confining his movement off the spot.

Slurps and gulps echoed against the walls as Stone hungrily fed on me. The feelings of pleasure caused only whimpers to escape my lips. My body screamed internally for mercy as I reached my peak. Bombs of insurmountable fulfillment detonated in my abdomen. Overwhelmed, a tear streamed from my eye and my fire hydrant burst, releasing torrents of gratification into his mouth. I was powerless and unable to inhale or exhale normally.

Stone rose and removed the eye covering, our eyes meeting while I tried to regain control of my breathing. His pole stood at full salute, beckoning me to put it at ease. He welcomed the heat of my saliva with a grunt.

"Shhh. Fuck." He moaned as I coursed my tongue along the top, bottom, and sides of his stake. I lured him back in inch by inch until I devoured his entire shaft. Demolishing his preliminary reward I became infatuated with getting the full compensation. Deep throating him to increase the juices that lubricated his pole, I quickened my pace, allowing his thickness to choke me. "Baby, slow down before you make a nigga bust." I honored his request, wanting to savor the moment, but couldn't resist the yearning I had to satisfy him. I hummed with each pull, causing vibrations in my throat while I applied the maximum pressure to draw out his syrupy treat.

"Nah. All my shooters are to make our seed." Seizing my arms, he lifted me and carried me to the living room floor.

Our tongues entangled violently as he sank down on the floor, gently placing me on the blanket sprawled out on the living room carpet. The heat from our bodies could have been ignition fluid for the fireplace we laid in front of. I spread my legs to give him the perfect view of how the clear lava in my pink volcano bubbled for him.

"You see what you do to me?" I asked, challenging him. The reflection of me in his pupils glistened like the stars in a night sky.

"Don't leave me no more," he said, kneeling down, stroking his tower of strength.

"This little piggy went to the market…" He used the nursery rhyme as he began drawing my big toe into his mouth and individually showed affection to each one.

"Baby, I can't take it. I need you inside of me. *Please*," I petitioned him.

"No, baby. I'm going to show attention to each area of your body tonight because I love every part of you." He was deliberately prolonging his entrance to provide me with intimacy.

Tracing his engorged rod around my inner pussy lips he tantalized me, making me crave him inside of me. He meticulously inserted only the tip of his head into my cave. The temptation was pushing me to a level of insanity.

"I can't take this shit. I need you, Stone," I cried.

He heeded my pleas and occupied my cave with his entire rod. Each slow, impassioned stroke breached a level of insecurity about the love we shared.

"Give yourself to me, Ma," Stone beckoned.

"I already have."

Locking myself onto him, I moved in sync with his thrusts, becoming one. My abyss of passion boiled over, ready to spew at any moment. Preparing to emit, I called for mercy, but it wasn't granted.

The plea stimulated him, causing each thrust to melt away my insides. No longer able to hold on, our explosions made their way to the top simultaneously, emitting magma.

Once we regained our strength he escorted me to the bathroom and directed me onto the edge of the tub. Squeezing out a small amount of bubble bath, he began the Jacuzzi. When enough water had filled the tub he slowly caressed my body with the sponge, showing affection to each part.

"Join me, baby," I invited.

"Nah, Krissett, tonight I'ma show you what you mean in my life."

He massaged my shoulders and feet before he allowed me to relax in the tub and then he went to our glass walk-in shower. We dried and lotioned every crevice of each other once we retreated into our bedroom for the night.

"Krissett, I need you to know you are the light in my world, Ma. Don't ever leave me again."

He made an effort to continue speaking, but I placed my finger onto his lips. "Shhh. Nothing needs to be said right now." There were no words that could prove what he had just shown me.

"Yeah, baby girl, there is. I want to apologize for all the bullshit in the past that I put you through. A nigga was out there thinking with the wrong head. I just want to love you."

"That's all I need from you."

"I need you to trust me with your heart. I promise it won't return broken." He planted a gentle kiss onto my forehead.

He embraced me tight and wrapped me in his legs. We dozed off to each other's breathing.

Stone healed my past wounds and made me believe in love I never thought possible. Words would only spoil the moment. If only temporary, I had faith that what he was giving me was finally the happiness I deserved.

Chapter 16

The sunlight shining through my blinds, along with the aroma of grits with cheese, cheese omelet, turkey bacon, and biscuits woke me up. I felt partially refreshed since Stone and I had hashed out our issue. It was time to handle the one with Meishelle.

Stone and I discussed it at the dining room table. There were no secrets between us, so he knew about Janasia. He played his usual role of devil's advocate, helping me to see the other side by posing possible arguments while remaining neutral in the overall decision. I wanted him to take my side, but I respected his honesty.

"So bae, after last night I think we need to get our wedding date together and get started on our family immediately," he motioned.

"I'm not tryna rush anything. We can take our time because once you take my hand in marriage, you're stuck with me," I answered with a smile in my eyes.

"I can deal with that. What's your plans for today?" Stone asked.

"My momma will have Na'Siah, so I planned time with Quincy and Meishelle to clear up this wedding beef we have going on. Other than that, nothing."

"I made plans for us to take a look at some things for the wedding. You down?" He asked.

"Always."

After we finished breakfast we got together and headed out.

***

Stone wouldn't tell me exactly what things we were going to look at, so I squirmed eagerly in the passenger seat.

Our first stop was an appointment at Swiss Confectionary, a popular cake bakery on St. Charles Avenue with the best cakes in the city. They had supplied all my cakes since I'd turned sixteen.

The cake designer asked several questions like cake type, wedding colors, and number of people we wanted to serve. I had waited so long for that moment. I described the dream cake I had seen in a wedding magazine. It was a five tier, boxed, white cake with buttercream icing, almond filling. It also had silver beading accents and the first letter of my new last name at the top.

It took about twenty minutes to arrive at the next destination, Ramsey's Diamond Jewelers. My face lit up like a Christmas tree. Everything was surreal. I was really getting married this time and Stone wanted to be involved in the process.

As he turned off the truck, Stone turned to me.

"You've never been big on jewelry, so I am bringing you here to make sure that I have a good idea of what you like. I'll make my final decision when I am ready to purchase it."

"Sure, bae. It's okay," I responded, smiling.

"Let me open your door again, hold tight." He was such a gentleman.

Walking inside, I felt star-struck at all the diamonds. I was far from broke, but jewelry had never been my thing. Clothes and shoes were my fetish, but this was definitely a new one that I would soon explore.

The grey haired sales lady greeted us, introducing herself as Jackie.

"Hey," Stone spoke up. "I think we spoke on the phone about looking at the engagement and wedding rings. I'm Gregory," he walked over to the counter extending his hand, "and this is Krissett."

"We certainly did. You are a gorgeous young couple. Right this way," she was starting in on her sales pitch already. She waved her hand toward the cases of our interests.

Placing his arm around my waist, we followed her lead.

My eyes glistened as I scanned the jewels in the case. I lit up like a sparkle myself. There were so many to choose from.

"What ring size are you?" Jackie asked.

"I'm not sure, to be honest," I replied.

She suggested we size my finger by trying on some rings. That sounded like a great idea to me.

The first ring I selected was a half karat, white gold ring, accented by twelve round cut diamonds. Holding my hand out in front of my face, I believed nail polish heightened the appearance of my hand, but it had nothing on a ring. It reinforced the idea that someone loved me enough to put a ring on it and verified I was wanted. Tears welled in my eyes as I continued to gaze at the rainbow that formed when the light hit the band. However, it was a little loose. We figured that I was a size seven, which Jackie said any ring could be sized if needed.

I continued to browse with Stone following me closely to see my next selection. In the next case I saw the one. The ring was absolutely stunning and screamed my name. I think Stone saw it in my eyes.

"That's the one isn't it?" He asked.

I was speechless. I could do nothing but nod. It was striking and looked more like a wedding ring than an engagement ring. I could wear it as either one with no problem. A total one and three fourths karats, it had a half karat, princess cut, center diamond, accented by twenty-two baguettes and forty round cuts. The shine as the light reflected off of it was blinding.

"I'm not sure. It doesn't look like one that you can band, honey, and I'm sure it's expensive. You would probably have to buy a whole new ring for our wedding day."

"I'm not concerned with the price or whether or not I have to buy another ring later. Money don't matter to me. You know better than that shit."

Jackie rejoined us. "So is there anything else you've found that you would like to look at?"

"That one, please," I smashed my finger over it in the case to make sure she picked up the right one.

"She has really good taste," Ms. Jackie said to Stone.

"That's one of the reasons I picked her." I blushed like a school girl daydreaming about her crush at the compliment.

"Here you go," she held it out.

Stone took the ring from her as I held out my finger for him. Tenderly taking my left hand with a grin on his face, he slipped the ring onto my finger. Planting a kiss on my cheek he said, "This is not even a part of what I want for us."

The tears that welled earlier trickled down my face. The ring fit like Cinderella's glass slipper.

"Perfect fit. It was made just for you," Stone said.

I didn't need to even ask the price. A blind man could see the ring was way too expensive. I was sure they had other rings that were more reasonable. We had a whole wedding to pay for so it made no sense to spend that kind of money on one ring and Stone would have to buy another. The realization that he thought I was worth marrying was worth far more to me than how much he spent on the ring itself. I pulled the ring off and told them that I wanted to keep looking.

"You sure about that?" Stone questioned me, skeptical of my answer.

"Absolutely," I assured him as I walked to another counter.

I viewed a few more rings that could be banded on our wedding day. Most of them would require sizing, but Jackie had that information. Stone also had an idea on what type of ring I wanted. I walked out of the store enthusiastic about what my future held, which was far different from a few years ago when I dreaded waking up to see another day. It was amazing how a good man held the power to change a woman's outlook on life.

My last surprise was a tour of the Botanical Gardens and New Orleans Museum of Arts in City Park. Stone wanted an outside wedding, but my fairytale wedding was to be inside at an exquisite venue. I wanted to allow for the worst case scenario, however, the park had many great features. It allowed versatility for everything to be done in one central location, the wedding portfolio, ceremony, and reception.

"So, baby what do you think?" I asked Stone.

"It's whatever you want. It's your day."

"It's yours as well, sir."

"True dat. As long as you become my wife and mother of my child the rest don't matter. The wedding is your day to show out."

"Aww, baby," I cooed as I planted a kiss on his cheek. "Your slick ass knows just what to say."

Don't Fu#k With My Heart

Chapter 17

Just as we were finishing up our day, my grandmother called and wanted us to bring her some Popeye's chicken. Stone had come in for a minute when I went inside to bring her the food. She went to the secret stash in her chair to retrieve money from a bank envelope.

"How many times have I told you about keeping money in this apartment instead of the bank?" She could be so stubborn when it came down to certain things.

"Girl, I can hold my own money. I don't know those people." she replied defiantly. "Was your phone broke that you couldn't answer it?" She asked, obviously not wanting to have that conversation.

"Grandma, people are too crazy for that nowadays." I wouldn't let her change the subject.

"You know what happened with the Great Depression, Krissett?" That was almost a century ago, but it was clear I wouldn't win this battle with her. She figured that she was obviously a threat to someone and she joked that if not she had me, Quincy, and Stone to take up for her. He chimed in his agreement, not helping the argument any. I noticed that her feet were swelling, a sign that she had stopped taking her fluid pills again. I cautioned her that she needed to watch that and take her medication, but I got the usual push back about that too. "Krissett, I raised you, not the other way around. I know how to take care of myself. How many years have I been here now?"

"Yes, ma'am," I said, shaking my head. "You need anything else?"

"Yes. I am cooking by your momma next Sunday for three o'clock. You and Stone need to be there."

She mentioned she would cook one of everyone's favorite dishes including Stone's. Stone replied, amped up. He knew Hattie Mae could throw down.

My phone rang, displaying Stone's grandmother's telephone number. I couldn't imagine what her conniving behind would want with me. Ever since she pulled that shit with Takeisha, Stone now attended his family events alone. I didn't give a fuck what it was.

"Where's your phone?" I rolled my eyes, handing the phone to Stone.

"In the car."

"You need to keep it on you for your family," I replied snidely.

He walked down the hallway to take the call and then asked me to come to the back for a minute. He told me his grandmother was calling for him to help her with the water bill for the month. Sewerage and Water Board had sent her a disconnection notice.

"Hell no!" I shouted. She had lost her damn mind. If she stayed out the casino she would be able to take care of her business. "I'm not even playing those type of games with your grandma."

"Krissett, this is my grandma, ma. I have to do this for her."

"Stone, she just got her check two days ago and the money is gone. Her house is paid for, so where did her money go? Plus, how could she run up a six hundred water bill? That means she hasn't paid it in months fooling with those damn card games."

"You serious right now?" He asked the question not believing I would deny his request. "Regardless, she needs water."

"Dead. We not supporting her habit. She wants our money to gamble. You not in the game anymore, so not here, she can't."

"I hear you," he replied, visibly upset.

Soon as me and my boo were getting back on track here she came with her nonsense as always. I was going to fix her lying ass. She must have forgotten I worked downtown with Entergy and had connections at Sewerage and Water Board. I was going to have her bill checked Monday morning to see what the balance and the status was. She wasn't gambling on my dime.

***

We changed our dinner plans when the skies turned dark and cloudy. I called my brother and we all decided on take-out at my house instead of going out. I didn't do anything in the rain.

Stone barely spoke to me on the way home other than saying what was necessary. *Shit didn't make any sense,* I thought to myself. His family would definitely be a topic of discussion before we tied the knot. By the time we picked up the food and liquor, Quincy and Meishelle were parked in the driveway waiting for us.

"Hey, lil' sis. What's up, Stone?" Quincy greeted while walking up the walk way.

He and Stone dapped each other and locked in a hug. Meishelle followed behind him.

"What's up, brother?" I continued to the door.

"You know me. I'm always good. Let me get those for you," he advanced his hand for the food bags.

"You would offer to get the food, greedy self."

"You know me," he grinned.

Quincy and I hardly ever had disagreements where we'd stop speaking, but when we did, whenever we hooked up again it was as if nothing had ever happened between us. We were each other's keepers, we couldn't keep away for too long.

Quincy and Stone started going in on the red beans and rice plates as soon as they hit the table. Giving them each their shot glasses, I placed Meishelle's in front of her.

"Thanks," she finally uttered.

"No problem," I said.

Quincy came up for air long enough to start the conversation. It seemed pretty clear that if he had left it to me or Meishelle there wouldn't be one.

"So, sis, you know we really want you in the wedding. Without a doubt we understand how you feel about Janasia, but we also have to respect Meishelle's family, especially her mother."

"Right, and I respect the decision which is why I removed myself. I have to look out for my best interest, but I thought about it and decided I would make this sacrifice for y'all.

"Me and Meishelle would never put you out there for a situation to occur. You know we are some of your biggest supporters."

"So when will you be fitted for your dress?" Meishelle asked with an evident attitude. She apparently wasn't as forgiving as Quincy had just been. If she didn't want to repair the friendship I would have to live with that. I would be in the wedding party just for my brother, but what she would not do is handle me.

"First off, you're in my house, so the attitude needed to be left at the door. I, by no means *have* to come back to the wedding party. It is a choice," I replied sharply.

138

"I don't have an attitude. I asked you a question, but no one is going to kiss your ass because you decided to come back to the wedding." Meishelle stated bluntly.

"I never asked for you to kiss anything on me. However, I can go get fitted during the week if you let me know when and where," I issued a rebuttal. Me and Meishelle never issued formal apologizes. It hadn't been necessary in our past disagreements so I didn't see the relevance of one now.

Quincy interjected to diffuse any possible situations while Stone remained silent.

"I'll text you the info. You're required to put down fifty percent, so they can order and begin the alterations."

"That's fine."

The table grew quiet as we all begin eating.

Finishing his food first, Quincy suggested we play dominoes. Once the game started the shit talking went well into the middle of the night. Me and Meishelle were back good a little while later. We had to have female unity to beat their asses on the table.

When my momma called to drop Na'Siah off, the game ended. Although it was late, Na'Siah came through the door smiling as usual. My mother was behind him with shopping bags in her hands.

"Hey, mommy's little man. Did you enjoy your day?"

"Yes. Nana took me to a birthday party and then shopping."

He was wired and full of energy. He bolted over to greet everyone.

Kissing my momma, I stepped aside for her to walk in with the shopping bags. "Y'all have a party going on in here, huh?"

Quincy and Stone rushed over to help her.

"Thanks fellas." She kissed each one of them. "I have to run, but make sure he is by Big Momma's at seven sharp. You know how she is."

"Yes, ma'am."

Since I had to be up so early, the party ended once my momma left. Hugging my brother and Meishelle, I watched them walk to the car, get in, and pull off.

Na'siah ran and tugged on my leg as Stone chased him. Those two were going to drive me crazy. I chuckled, imagining how the house would be with Stone, Na'Siah, and our little one on a permanent basis. My three running around, screaming, and bonding together, toys scattered all around the floor and constantly having to clean up behind them. Thinking about it made me realize how much I loved my life and that I wouldn't trade it for a million dollars.

Chapter 18

Throwing on my multi-colored, silk, halter maxi, sundress, I was finally ready for Hatti Mae's party. My week had gone smoothly, both on the work and home front. It had been quite some time since that had happened. Stone was growing concerned about being late for the meal my grandmother invited us to attend. My momma lived in an upscale neighborhood less than five minutes from my house.

"Babe, come on. We gon' be late," he rushed me, worried the food wouldn't last long.

I was stepping into my five inch, hot pink, Jimmy Choo rope sandals.

"If you wouldn't have wanted that makeup shower session we wouldn't be running late," I eyed him devilishly. I went back on my original decision to loan his grandmother the money. I suggested to Stone that we just make the water bill payment ourselves instead of giving her the money. I knew the bill wasn't that much so I would expose her for being a liar.

Seeing he was about to have a fit, I decided to put on my accessories and makeup on the way.

Grandma must have invited all of our family members from generations past. Cars were lined up and down my mother's block. She had a gorgeous two-story, five bedroom home that included an entertainment room, large patio, and back yard. She had the dream home I wanted one day. Only her house could accommodate our huge family.

Unfortunately, that included Mariah. Out of respect for Craig, she was invited to family gatherings which she always managed to make with Quameer by her side. While the family tolerated her, they looked down on Mariah with disdain for the way she handled the situation. Her mom and my step-dad, Craig, shared custody, so as a child she spent equal time at our house as well as her mom's. She always had ill feelings toward my mom, believing that she'd stolen her dad from her mother. That was far from the truth.

Her parents had been separated for over five years before Craig and my mom started dating. She was young and still holding onto the hope of her parents reconciling. Since I had her dad on a full time basis, I assumed jealously and her thirst for revenge set in. Thus she began by taking Quameer, my sloppy seconds. I had never seen it coming.

One would swear Quameer treated a woman like a queen, but his multiple baby mommas told the truth about him. He never stayed with one woman or paid his child support because he couldn't hold down a job. I handled it for him when we were together and I assumed Mariah did the same to keep his ass out of jail. Men like that couldn't ever get ahead so he preyed on hard working women who would take care of him. I tried to warn Mariah as my last sisterly act, but she wouldn't listen. Instead, she played a role in convincing Quameer to take my son. It was true, family would stab you in the back quicker than a stranger on the street.

I went straight into the kitchen while Stone joined the men in the entertainment room. The table was set outside on the patio, buffet style. There were red beans, butter beans, macaroni and cheese, loaded baked potatoes, stuffed peppers, ham, roast beef, green beans, greens, cornbread and dinner rolls. Desserts of all kinds lined the counter top. They also had a few sacks of crawfish with potatoes, corn, and turkey necks for those who didn't want the big plates. Hot dogs, hamburgers, and nachos were for the kids.

"What's going on over here? Something I need to know?" I entered the kitchen.

"No, baby," Grandma spoke up. "We hadn't come together in a while so we threw this together."

"Why didn't anyone ask me to bring anything?" I asked.

"No one bought anything. Me and Craig took care of everything. I just asked Momma to cook and your cousin, Josh, to boil," my momma answered.

"Oh, okay then. Where do I get in?" I knew I had an assignment waiting for me.

"Start taking these pans outside and put them over the sternos," my aunt handed me a pan.

"Okay," I grabbed pans one by one as I headed outside.

About thirty minutes later everything was set up. Grandma called everyone outside to say grace before anyone so much as picked up a plate. After finishing grace my momma had everyone grab a glass of champagne.

"I would like to make a toast to family, our existing and future members. Welcome," she lifted her glass.

"To family," everyone chanted in unison and clicked their glasses together.

Stone's mother, grandmother, and family joined in at the patio door. They must have been in the dining room with everyone else so I hadn't seen them. His grandmother wore her usual frown. *Why is her ass even here?* I wondered.

"Since we are all together I wanted to do this right," Stone announced, grabbing my hand and pulling me toward the front of the crowd. My heartbeat sped up thinking about what he was about to do. Facing out to them on the patio he continued, "This woman has stood by my side through it all and I love her." He got down on his knee, "It's time we make this official."

He pulled the ring box out of his back pocket, "Come here, Na'Siah." He motioned for him to come from Quameer. Everyone stepped aside to allow him to pass. "So,

Krissett and Na'Siah, will you have me?" He opened the box revealing my Cinderella ring from Ramsey's. I gasped as my eyes beheld the ring. The answer got lodged in my throat as tears welled in my eyes.

"Yes, we do." Na'Siah hugged his neck. Everyone broke out into laughter.

"What about you, Krissett?" He joked.

I nodded my head *yes*. My momma, grandmother and Meishelle shrieked as he grabbed my left hand and glided the ring on to it. Standing up, he placed a passionate kiss on my lips.

"Now let's eat," he rejoiced.

Mine and Quincy's family members congratulated me with the exception of his grandmother, which surprised me in no way. My four favorite ladies waited until everyone else finished and then rejoined me.

"Now we can plan your wedding," Meishelle yelled.

"Yep. Some of the details I already have. We started last weekend," I snickered.

Na'Siah came back for something to eat after he had run off with his cousin. Grabbing my hand to bring him to the table for his plate he said, "Ooh, mommy, your ring is pretty."

"You like it?"

"Yep," he answered, bobbing his head up and down.

The deejay arrived about twenty minutes later and set it off. My momma and grandmother confessed that this was my engagement party. They planned it while I had been in Atlanta. Even Schtanya had come down with her family. I should have known something was up when I saw her there.

"Congrats cousin," she hollered excitedly.

"You deserve this, baby," my momma said proudly.

144

"Sure do. My baby's about to become a wife," Grandma added.

"You are up next," Meishelle chimed in.

Starting their respective card games of Pitty Pat and Tonk, everyone enjoyed themselves until they heard the brass tuba, trumpet, and other instruments coming through.

Only in New Orleans did we second line for any and every occasion. With Stone's cousin handing me my decorated umbrella of teal blue and silver panels with a huge bow, we paraded around the back yard for the next thirty minutes. All that was missing to complete the jubilee were the people who dressed in elaborate Indian costumes. If this was just the engagement party, I couldn't imagine the rehearsal dinner or wedding.

As everyone filed out, they expressed how much they enjoyed themselves, giving me a second batch of congrats until Stone's grandmother's turn came.

"I'll never recognize you as a member of the Robertson family," she smugly proclaimed.

"You don't have to, Mrs. Miriam. As long as Stone does I'll be fine," I respectfully applied.

"You're a damn fool if you ever think my grandson will only be with you. There will always be another and I will welcome her with open arms," she spat, full of hate.

"Well, for now I'm the one with the ring, so it looks like your wrong," I was trying to remain respectful to my elder, but she was pushing it.

"Your looney ass can't take care of your own son. How can you ever be a decent wife?"

Now she had gone too fucking far. I'd remained as civil as I possibly could on the strength of Stone, but she deserved no respect. That miserable ass old lady would know after that day to walk in the other direction if she saw me coming down the street.

"Hear me very well when I say this," I inched as close to her as I could without making a scene. "Your gold digging behind was the one who put me on Stone to begin with. You didn't raise your own damn kids tricking in the street, your mother did. So before you cast any stones, take a good look in the mirror because it takes a crazy person to know one. Now mess with me and let's see who's crazier." When it came to her, I had every intention of keeping my promises.

Stone came up behind me and kissed my cheek. "Hey, Grams. We will have that money to you on tomorrow for the water bill."

"Oh my, baby," she kissed Stone on the cheek. "I love y'all both so much for always helping me out." I pondered whether or not she was bi-polar. "I'll see you tomorrow when you bring it to me." Little did she know, he would never arrive with it.

Bright and early in the morning I stood in the line at Sewerage and Water Board with my checkbook to pay her account. A middle age lady offered her assistance.

"Good Morning. How can I help you?" The lady greeted me.

"I would like to make a six hundred dollar payment on the account of Mrs. Miriam Robertson, eighteen oh five Charbonnet Street, please."

The lady looked through her account information on the computer. "I'm sorry. The account balance is nowhere near that high to make a payment of that amount."

"Ok. Thank you." A smile a mile long graced my face. I couldn't wait to tell Stone this.

10:05 a.m.: The lady at the water company says the bill is no way near the amount your grandma is asking for. You sure she said $600?

10:06 a.m.: WTF? I'm positive that's what she said.

10:07 a.m.: So what you want me to do?

10:08 a.m.: Go ahead and leave. I'll handle it on lunch.

10:09 a.m.: Gotcha.

I smirked thinking about how the conversation between Stone and his grandmother would go. I was sure it would make her blood boil. I despised the fact that she would risk keeping her grandson in the game to have a more comfortable life instead of thinking about the possibility that he could end up in a black fucking box. As I walked out of the service center, I knew my week would be great.

Don't Fu#k With My Heart

Chapter 19

Stone came home Wednesday with a texted picture of a lesbian for our threesome. His cousin had sent a picture of one of her cut buddies. She had a nice body and good looks based on what he showed me. Never had I looked at a chick sexually, but I was willing to give a girl her props when she deserved them. Standing about five feet, three inches, she was red skinned with button shaped brown eyes. Her hair was worn in short, tight curls. She had a little bit more weight than me in the breasts, but not in the hips or butt.

She called me the following week, assuming Stone had given her my number for a meet and greet. She wanted to meet at Rainbow Lanes, the bowling alley in Kenner. I hadn't bowled in quite a minute, so I welcomed the offer. I agreed to meet her that Wednesday after work.

The only thing I disliked about spring was it always seemed to rain, especially in April. The weather was so ugly that day I almost cancelled, but the rain subsided so I kept the plans.

"Krissett," she called out as I approached the bowling alley.

"Cionna?" I needed to verify if it was her.

"The one and only," she answered, identifying herself.

She wore a black chiffon shirt with a white bra underneath, black and white checker print tights that hugged her figure, and a pair of teal iridescent pumps. The pictures didn't show enough of her shape. The chick was bad, much like myself.

She greeted me with a hug and a smile as she eyed my body from head to toe. "How are you today?"

"I'm okay and you?" I replied as we walked into the alley. In a nervous rush I asked her another question without allowing her to answer the first one. "What made you pick bowling?"

She giggled, "I'm good and I was told the rule was a public spot and this is something I enjoy doing. You ever bowled before?"

"Yeah, but it's been a while."

We rented the lane for a few games and got our shoes. I wasn't in a hurry since nothing waited for me at home.

"She went to the bar and returned with two drinks in her hand, "Sorry, I don't like to drink alone," she returned with a Heineken for me. "I left the cap on just so you know I didn't do anything to it."

Beer wasn't my choice of alcohol, but rather than blow her down I decided to drink it as a courtesy.

"I hope you don't mind that I already went first," she'd made a strike.

"Nope, not at all." I went to the lane for my turn. I knocked down four pins on my first try and the gutter took my ball on the second.

"So, tell me a little about yourself," Cionna probed.

I filled her in on me, telling her that I was twenty-eight and that Stone was my fiancé. I also told her that I had one son and two best friends, and that shopping was my hobby. She returned that she was thirty, no man, woman, or kids, and a few friends.

"So, why a threesome?"

"Stone asked for one, basically."

"Well, damn! It's that easy?" She laughed. "I don't mean any harm. So, what about you? Have you ever been interested in women? I've heard every woman's fantasy is another woman."

"I'm not easily offended, but no it wasn't easy. It took a lot of thought as I don't trust females or men. And as far as a female fantasy, I have never, ever considered that kind of get down."

"Understood. It's such a shame though, because you might like being with a woman."

"Can't miss what you never had," I shot her offer down, getting up to go to the snack bar.

Our girl talk continued on smoothly once the boundaries had been established. She was from Memphis, Tennessee and moved to New Orleans for a job, but lost it shortly after she arrived. I asked what the deal was with her and Stone's cousin. She said they had an understanding that when either one was horny they would hook up. There was no commitment because she was very comfortable being alone. She had, so far, met all the stipulations I laid forth and the more time I spent with her the more I began to feel an attraction to her which stunned me. Maybe it was the fact that in my mind I was picturing me, her, and Stone getting it in. We got about four games in before the lanes shut down.

Not ready to go just yet, she invited me into the bar area for a few more drinks. She mentioned that she had been with men at one time, but got tired of the consistent issues that came with them. The serious relationships she had been in with women ended on mutual terms because they realized they only had sex in common, which was why she was single.

The conversation went on for about an hour before we decided to leave. As we headed out, I told her I would be in touch for a sit down dinner with Stone within the next few weeks. If they were compatible, then we could arrange a date for the threesome. She said that she was down. *I must really love this man to even be considering this,* I thought as I shook my head while I watched her walk away.

***

After weeks of practice and using ovulation test for calculation, I had yet to get pregnant. Stone wasn't tripping, but out of curiosity I made an appointment with a fertility specialist. Dr. Gregory Coleman was a doctor that came highly recommended.

The nurse placed me in the room after taking my vitals. "The doctor will be right with you."

He must have been right outside the door because he barged through the moment she finished.

"Hello, Ms. Baptiste, nice to meet you," he reached out to shake my hand with a smile.

He was an older, black doctor, maybe in his mid-fifties with slight greying around his front hairline, and a perfect smile. He was extremely handsome and it was obvious he had kept himself up. I guess with the money he made it was easy.

He greeted me and explained that he would collect some medical information and order some tests based on our conversation. Then we would arrange a follow up appointment if I chose to do so. I needed to know what was going on so I agreed.

"What brings you in today?"

"Well, me and my fiancé are trying to have a baby and it hasn't happened yet."

"Okay. Let's see if there's a problem and if so, how we can fix it. I'll go over the medical history you gave on the new patient paperwork and ask some questions. I see you have one son who is five years old. Natural child birth. Slightly premature. You also mention a history of chlamydia. Just one time?"

"Yes, sir." *Fucking around with Quameer and Janasia's stank asses,* I thought. It always seemed to make me feel nasty and like a fool.

To many people assumed that the woman had always contracted it from sleeping around.

Sensing my feelings he said, "It's okay. Things happen to the best of us." He attempted to smooth it over with me. I nodded my head. "I see here you also have irregular cycles. What I will do is order you some blood work to check some levels and an HSG test. I should have the blood work back in about two days, okay?"

"Okay, thank you."

"No problem," he said, rising from the chair.

He wanted me to have an HSG test due to my STD history, it was a test I had never heard of before. We would also make an appointment to do a transvaginal ultrasound and check the size of my eggs. He wanted to eventually have Stone come in and check his sperm levels, but that damn sure wasn't going to happen.

That night, since Stone was working, I had time to do my own research. I had never heard of HSG, but I definitely wanted to know what the hell it was. It was a test commonly used to determine blocked tubes. Apparently when a woman had an STD for an extended period of time, tissue would form around her fallopian tubes to block the infection from spreading, rendering her infertile.

Covering my mouth, I dashed down the hall, barely making it to the bathroom. Seemed like everything I had for breakfast, lunch, and dinner came out in those minutes. That couldn't be possible.

Since I didn't know what the deal really was, I wasn't going to tell anyone, not even Meishelle. This would be my only and best kept secret.

Don't Fu#k With My Heart

Chapter 20

A few days later was D-day for my fertility question. The HSG test was the last step in the process to creating me and Stone's seed. After performing the ultrasounds, Dr. Coleman prescribed me Clomid, a medication designed to help my follicles grow. He said once the test came back negative I could begin to take them.

I decided to take the scenic route by way of the trolley, our above ground electrical train system. The tracks and electrical lines allowed the system to operate throughout the city. On days when I yearned for serenity, I would catch it for a round trip.

About nine that morning I parked my car at Canal Place, the small upscale shopping mall located at the base of Canal Street.

The outdoor train whistled along the neutral ground track that divided St. Charles Ave. Opening my window, the huge, old oak trees seemed to pass by in slow motion, or maybe it was my nervousness that made time move like a snail.

When I arrived at my stop I still had to walk up the block to Diagnostic Imaging. An uneasy feeling rose inside me when I entered. My hands shook as I tried to force them to sign the sign in sheet. After presenting my insurance card, I was immediately called to the back. The nurse directed me to a bathroom in the testing room to undress and place on a hospital gown with my back out.

Coming out of the room, my body trembled as I willed my legs to the table. Lying down, the ice cold, stainless steel slab sent chills surging through my body as I eased myself onto the table. The radiologist entered the room and introduced himself.

"Hello, Ms. Baptiste. I'm William. I'll be performing your test."

"Okay," I responded, looking straight up at the ceiling.

"I'm going to walk you through the procedure and then we will get started."

"Uh huh," I said.

I heard little to none of the directions before he asked if I was ready.

"I guess so," I said, taking a deep breathe.

The room was freezing but I was perspiring profusely. The table became almost slippery until I thought I would just trail off. My heart beat was so intense I could hear it pulsing and coursing through my head. I placed my hands across my stomach, instantly dampening the gown.

"Okay. Now you have to relax your muscles so I can insert the tube. "There will be a slight burn. Try to think nice thoughts."

Easy for your ass to say, I thought to myself. I had no sensation as numbness had taken over my lower extremity at that point.

"Here is the dye. You can look at the screen and we will see."

"I don't know what I'm really looking at," I responded, turning my head toward the wall. I repeated the Our Father prayer throughout the short procedure. Those two minutes seemed like two hours.

The distress in his face gave the results before his mouth could. Shaking his head, he said, "I'm sorry, Ms. Baptiste. The dye did not go through. It appears they're blocked."

I lay on the table, emotionless. He reached his hand out to help me off, but I didn't move. My chest heaved and my mouth gaped for air to enter. My arms limply hung, having lost all voluntary muscle control, my mind scrambled to process the news. As it came to terms with each word, my hopes and dreams shattered like glass dishes falling to the floor repetitively. I wanted to die. I would never be able to give my husband a family of his own. Never give Na'Siah the brother or sister he asked me to have.

My mental scrambled to recall what I could have done to be punished in such a manner. Every time I tried to heal, the past resurfaced to remind me of how unfair life could be. This wasn't my sin, but I bore all the consequences. Both of my teenage loves had allowed another bitch to steal my ability to bring life into this world. Hollow's woman stomped life out of my womb and Quameer robbed me by transmitting an STD to me from Janasia. Now they would affect my fairy tale ending with Stone.

"I'll go get you some water and give you a few minutes. I'm terribly sorry," William sincerely apologized as he exited the room.

Prying my body off of the table, I went into the bathroom and stared at myself in the mirror. I watched the tears pour down my face in massive amounts. My living seemed to be in vain because I suffered each and every day I continued to exist. Then I heard a knock at my door.

"Ms. Baptiste, are you okay in there? You left your clothes out here."

"I'll be out in a minute," I sniffled back my tears and runny nose.

"Okay. I'll step out, but I'll check on you again shortly."

I waited a moment before I stepped out and grabbed my clothes off of the chair, then I retreated back into the bathroom. I sat on the toilet because I felt drained and void of energy. Sliding on my blouse, I used the metal rail to pull myself up and steady my balance. Peeking out of the door I noticed there was no nurse. I grabbed my purse and quickly headed out of the location before I lost complete control of my emotions.

***

Gazing up, I had walked several blocks to gain enough composure for the ride back. Gaining slight control of my eye faucets for a few minutes, I caught the approaching trolley. I laid my head back, pleading with the grim reaper to collect me. Those people didn't know me so they wouldn't dare save me. Instead time sped up, causing the ride to be quicker since there were not many people to make stops for.

Sending a quick text to Stone that I would be working late, I rode the trolley in the opposite direction of home for a five flavor daiquiri with two shots of Patron. I wanted to be comforted by my man, but I couldn't tell him. My frozen alcohol treat would have to console me instead.

Riding back to the car, I endeavored to drown my sorrows in the alcohol, but to no avail. Arriving back to my original stop, I wandered aimlessly toward the Riverfront. Sitting on the edge of the Mississippi River bank, the water presented a permanent solution to my impending problem.

I looked down at the rock that graced my hand as the red and orange sky line drew the day, and possibly my life, to a close. Tears streamed down my face. The moving river water displayed my dreams in the reflection. Stone encouraging me as the doctor instructed me to push, his proud father smile holding our baby and bringing him inside from the hospital.

Stone was entitled to a loyal wife that would give him all his heart's desires. How was I ever going to crush that man's dreams and tell him I couldn't have his baby? He had restored me, made me whole again. He was my King. He made

158

my story ending one that was happily ever after. From my experience, men like him came a dime a dozen and I wasn't willing to take the risk of losing him.

My heart felt as if it was being rung out like a soaking towel. Each twist caused more wrenching agony. All my mind would allow me to do was focus on all the horrid things that had happened in my life. The good seemed to be few and far between. I wondered if I would ever get a chance to be truly happy.

By the time I walked in my home, my plan was to head straight to the medicine cabinet. Pills, patron, bath, and the bed. I had to get up extra early because Hattie Mae called me on my way home, asking me to bring her to the doctor the next day.

Passing the spare bedroom we kept for company, my mind began playing tricks on me. I envisioned the daughter I would have had stretched across the bed laughing while surfing Facebook on her cellphone. She would be a freshman in high school by now. She would be fair skinned and tall like Hollow, somehow managing to get grey eyes instead of hazel like mine.

"Mom," she called out to me as I walked down the hall.
"Yeah, baby," I responded.
"I need an outfit for the movies this weekend. Can you take me shopping Saturday?"
"All the clothes you have in there? You better find something."
"Ughh! I'll just ask Grandma," she whined.

Walking further, I reached Na'Siah's room and everything fell apart for me. I sat on his bed holding his teddy bear close to my heart. A new baby would've allowed me to enjoy the most precious moments I'd missed with Na'Siah due to the absent mindedness caused by my mania.

Lying in my bed, I could hear Na'Siah's screams through the thin walls. I had lost count of the days since the police told me Quameer had deserted us. I staggered down the hallway with him, making it as far as the bathroom doorway before nausea took over my insides. Placing my head deep in the toilet, my body convulsed, stomach muscles aching as I hurled out alcohol and pills, the only contents of my stomach. Gripping the toilet bowl, my arms burned from the superficial cuts I had inflicted too numb the pain in my heart.

Dragging my body out of the bed hours later, I found him standing in the crib. His eyes were red from the blood vessels that had busted because of his constant screams. He hollered even louder from the red bumps on his behind.

"Mommy is so sorry, but I have to change you." I pleaded for his forgiveness. "I didn't mean it, I promise." I had left him unchanged for far too long, losing count of the days. Sitting him in his high chair, he hungrily gobbled down the food in the apartment, choking on the first few bites.

Holding onto the bedroom wall, I lost my balance and fell into the bed face first. Retrieving two Lithium and taking a swig from the Jack Daniel's bottle, I threw my head back. It singed my throat and entered into my digestive tract. Before they could work, Na'Siah broke the silence with his cries.

"Please son, I need you to be quiet." He only got louder, stabbing at my heart. I rocked back and forth, crying hysterically, begging him to please stop. Reaching for him I found that his body was burning up and I felt for his arm which he was using to grab at his ear.

The idea that my baby was suffering at my expense set fire to my heart. My chest throbbed. Only a low down mother would allow her baby to get down to this state. I kept falling into depressions and the one who agonized was him. I couldn't live like this.

I shoved many as Lithium as I could inside of my mouth, chasing them down with a gulp of liquor. I gagged as my body tried to refuse them and hold onto the life I was trying to suck out of it. I lay back covering my head, praying that everything finally went silent, including Na'Siah.

A few minutes later I called my mother. "Momma, please come get him. I'm hurting him," I pleaded with her.

"What do you mean Krissett? Why is he screaming like that?" She panicked.

"I don't know. He's burning up. I don't have the strength to get up, but something is wrong with him." Tears streamed down my face onto the sheets. I was losing consciousness, the pills fulfilling their deadly mission.

The phone fell from my hand as I heard her frantic cries.

Don't Fu#k With My Heart

Chapter 21

Downing four or my mania medication before I lay down for the night, Stone found me crying and hurling my guts up into a bucket.

"Babe, what's going on?" He was concerned.

"Must be coming down with a stomach virus," I lied.

"You sure it's not something else," he grinned.

"Yeah, I'm sure. I just had my yearly checkup," I told a second lie.

His excitement from thinking that I might be pregnant made me feel even worse. I felt so low down for keeping the truth from him, but I couldn't just come out and say it. I despised a deceitful person, but I was becoming one more and more with each untruth I told. I justified my actions by telling myself that I was still trying to deal with the devastating news.

Joining me on my side, he wrapped his arms and legs around and pulled me into a tight bear hold.

"I got you, ma" he whispered, kissing the back of my neck.

He was helping to mold an entirely new self-image of who I was. What I saw as an unattractive, blue, long nosed muppet character named Gonzo in junior high was transforming into a sexy, beautiful woman. Inside and out was coming together. There were options, but none that would allow our seed to be entirely ours. I wanted my baby to have both of our DNA running through their body, but I had just lied, so surgery or any other alternate methods would expose my sterility and make the situation worse.

The lighting of the sky meant time was moving by. When the cable box reflected six in the morning, my head pounded, the room spun, and the nausea was extreme. I drug myself to the bathroom using the small amount of the light from the other rooms. I had learned through years of practice to smile through all of the pain. My ability to hide feelings was as close to perfection as possible.

Selecting a jogging suit and matching tennis shoes, I quickly showered and dressed by candlelight. I had a full day ahead despite me feeling like shit. Half the day with Hattie Mae, the other part getting the final fitting for my dress, and a day spa followed by the gym. Anything that could occupy my mind was much welcomed.

After a brutal morning commute to pick my grandmother up, she came straight out, cane in hand. Good thing her doctor visits never took long.

After the appointment she wanted to head to Harrah's Casino by the Riverfront. I cursed myself for taking those pills, knowing I hadn't eaten a thing. I wanted to take a nap in the garage while she went in, but that would have been a dead giveaway.

Once inside she headed to her favorite machines, the nickel shots. She would always hit and had a billion points she could use for all types of things. She'd often used them to comp me and Stone's rooms when we went on vacation and also to treat the whole crew to Friday night dinners. Seeing that she was in her glory there, I headed to my beloved game, craps.

I was up by a hundred and relishing in my winning streak when the scent of Polo Black surrounded me and I felt *his* hands cover my eyes.

"Guess who?" The deep voice that I instantly recognized vibrated in my eardrum and I wasn't sure why he was here, especially right then.

"Hollow," I exhaled in exasperation. He was one of the last people I wanted to see.

"Don't sound so excited about it." He moved to my side at the table. "How are you?"

"Not in the mood for you," I replied sharply. If it wasn't for his stupid ass baby momma I would have my baby girl and boy right now.

"Damn, love. You have to forgive me at some point, right?"

"Who told you that lie?" I temporarily took my focus off the table.

"I'm trying to make right for my wrong, why won't you let me?"

"Let you how, Hollow? You are not welcome back into my world. You've fucked it up enough." I was trying to keep the conversation quiet, but he was pushing it.

"How, Krissett? We didn't get a chance to talk much at the mall."

"It was on purpose," I stopped him with my hand. "I have way too much shit I'm dealing with."

"I just want the chance to actually apologize for what happened." It was evident he was going to persist. I would have given anything for a gun at that moment. I would have blown that muthafucka's brain out without remorse. Life for a life.

"Apologies never replace a life, Hollow, so it doesn't hold much weight."

"True dat, but at least try to let me make it right, Krissett."

"Someone already has," I flashed my rock.

"That don't mean shit. I've given my share of those too."

"I hear you," I picked up my chips to leave the table.

I hoped my grandmother was ready to go. Hollow had completely ruined my chance at stress relief.

"Where you headed?" He had never been a stalker, but today he damn sure fit the profile.

"To find my grandmother and to cash in these chips."

"Oh, snap, my girl is in here? Why you didn't tell me?" I questioned what the fuck would make me tell him.

"What would have been the reason for me to?" I said smugly.

"Because she's my heart."

"That's too fucking lame," I had to laugh at this clown.

It took fifteen minutes to find Hattie Mae, she was notorious for getting lost in the casino. As we searched, he rambled on about shit I couldn't give fuck about. He talked about a job he had gotten in the city and was in the process of moving back. I told him a couple of areas he could check out and places to lay. He invited me and Hattie Mae to lunch one day but I told him to talk to her about that. She would be attending alone. It was highly likely that she would accept seeing as she loved to eat and didn't hold grudges. I wouldn't dare speak up for her, though.

Finally we found her at the Wheel of Fortune machine. Hollow playfully covered her eyes too. When she saw who it was she hollered so loud a few patrons mistook her screams for her hitting the jackpot.

"Hey, my baby. It's been forever. How have you been?" She could make anybody feel loved.

"I've been good, Ms. Hattie Mae. How are you? I asked Krissett about you a few weeks back."

"She mentioned it to me, but nothing like actually laying eyes on you. You look like life has treated you well."

"It's definitely handling me. Not sure how well, though," he laughed.

"What you doing with yourself?"

"I just got a manager job at Ruth Chris' Steak House in here, so I'm moving back home soon."

"That's wonderful. I'm sure your family will be happy about that."

"Maybe," he shrugged. "How about I take you and Krissett out to lunch sometime."

"You can certainly take me, but with Krissett it depends on how her fiancé feels about it. You know I respect relationships."

"We good with or without her," he replied.

"You bet we good."

Helping her up from her chair, they walked, arms locked, to the cash out booth. Catching up on times, they decided to have lunch right then. Since I had made other appointments Hollow agreed to bring my grandmother home. Those two together would be an all-day affair. He had a special place in her heart, he was the son she never had. She met him once I revealed I was pregnant and took him under her wing. All he had was an aunt around. I believe he broke her heart as much as mine when everything went down. She just held hers back to remain strong for me.

I headed to Metairie, which was ten minutes outside of New Orleans, to David's Bridal for my dress. The alterations to my maid of honor dress was perfect. The red, off shoulder, floor length, peplum style gown with a small train hugged me in all the right places. I couldn't wait for the wedding day. It was hard to believe the wedding was only a couple of weeks away. After Quincy and Meishelle's wedding, I hoped I could only be the matron of honor in any future matrimonies. I briefly considered looking around for my own wedding gown, but dismissed the idea after my news yesterday. I had no idea what the hell my future had in store.

Looking at my watch, I was glad I had scheduled my spa day for two that afternoon. I would get there in just enough time. I had reserved the Ultimate Spa experience which included everything.

Arriving, I made sure to grab my iPod to listen to my own music. The warm water on my feet as the turbine caused the water to bubble felt great. The balls in the chair rubbed against my back. A bowl of warm water was placed on my lap for my hands. My tension began to evaporate through the water. The whole experience was one of a kind and there was no doubt I would be back again for that service. There was even a package for Stone, although he would probably turn me down. He felt things like that weren't masculine.

Leaving the spa, I almost felt better until I saw a lady jogging down the street with a baby on her shoulder. I cursed at her in my mind while jealously and rage filled me. Every ounce of tension the spa had just worked out of me returned in an instant. Another moment I would never have because of the recklessness of others.

Chapter 22

I avoided public places for the next few weeks. The more women I saw with their babies, the more shooting pains I felt in my chest and I couldn't hold back the tears. My energy depleted and my muscles weakened from the daily regimen of nerve pills, opiates, and alcohol I pumped into my system. My only coping mechanism was to be far away from reality. Weekends were the only time I was sober and that was only for Na'Siah.

Stone did everything he could to cheer me up, but nothing worked. I wanted to share the news with him, but the thought of having to look him in the eyes I couldn't take. Out of options, he contacted my psychologist who called me to make an appointment. She stressed the importance of her being able to give a good report about me for the upcoming court date. I assured her I was fine, but she insisted that I come in for an appointment as soon as possible. Making myself seem extra busy at work, I arranged one for the following month.

Cionna texted me that she would be leaving in about a week to return to Tennessee because her mother has been recently diagnosed with cancer. Since she knew I was going to hit her up about us having dinner, she asked if we wanted to do it before she left. The threesome was definitely the last thing on my mind, but I told myself I needed to push through this for Stone. It was the least I could do. We decided to eat at Copeland's.

"You look beautiful," Stone kissed me on the cheek as we walked into the restaurant.

"Thanks, baby. You look pretty sexy yourself," I repaid the compliment.

Cionna was sitting in the seating area waiting for us. We shared a hug before I did the introductions.

"Nice to meet you," Stone offered his hand to be shaken.

"The pleasure is mine," she accepted. "I've heard a lot about you."

While they placed their orders, I requested a drink with alcohol called the Crash & Burn.

"Babe, why don't you at least get an appetizer?" Stone invited.

My appetite had been scarce with all the medications and I could see it in my clothing.

"I'm ok, babe. I ate a sandwich for lunch."

"Well I'll order some jazzy wings and we can share them," he insisted.

The connection was good between them and conversation flowed freely on various topics. I chimed in to lay out my full expectations in the threesome. There was to be no contact between them outside of me, that was most important. Otherwise, I only jumped in every now and then to seem somewhat involved as they continued to talk over the food.

She asked me if I could help her get on at my job and I asked her for a resume. I would hand it off to a recruiter, but I wasn't pulling any of my strings. We weren't that damn cool. We agreed to have the threesome a week after she returned from Tennessee to give her a chance to get settled.

"See you later. You take care of yourself," I wished her well.

"I definitely will." She hugged us both before we walked to our car.

Stone locked my arm in his as we strolled down the block to the vehicle. "I know you must have some apprehensions, but I appreciate you doing this for me more than you can imagine. You definitely hold a nigga down," he earnestly stated.

"You know I got my boo all day long. I've put my trust in you and the fact that I believe you will always do right by me." I spoke from my heart. I no longer felt the need to check his cell phone records or doubt anything that he said. Actions spoke louder than words and his had demonstrated his feelings.

"No doubt, ma. Nigga love you for that shit too.

Like most nights we went home and made passionate love to make a baby that could never be.

Don't Fu#k With My Heart

Chapter 23

Stone requested off the night of the rehearsal to take me and Na'Siah out to eat. Na'Siah wanted his favorite restaurant, Golden Corral. As a later part of our agreement between me and the couple, I would only participate in the wedding. This would limit the amount of contact I had with Janasia. As a slight work around it, they used Photoshop to include me and the best man, Jamal, on some of the engagement pictures.

Checking my appearance in the mirror for the wedding ceremony, I downed my new regularly scheduled drugs to suppress my system. I needed to ensure I would remain as lax as possible. Just in case they begin to wear off, I placed a few extra in the small handbag that dangled from my wrist.

My weight loss showed. Where my dress once hugged my curves it was now loose, including in the chest area which was only slightly noticeable to the naked eye. My girl, Mika, had hooked my hair up in a pin up style similar to a messy bun with perfect makeup. I looked a mess in my eyes, but it would have to work.

Stone walked up behind me in the mirror. "You look beautiful, baby." He pulled me into an embrace and planted a kiss on the side of my neck.

"Thanks, boo." I freed myself from him. "You ready?"

"Yeah. I don't really know what the deal is with you, but I wish you would just tell me."

"It's nothing, boo. I'm cool. Just thinking about how this shit will go today with Janasia. I'm not for the foolishness," I hunched my shoulders.

"There's nothing to worry about. No matter what, I got you," he reassured me.

I couldn't hold this shit in much longer. "Baby, I have something we need to talk about. Have a seat," I patted the bed.

"If it's anything about us we're fine until we get home tonight. I want you to just relax and enjoy this day."

"As soon as we get home, though. Deal?" I waited for him to accept.

"Deal," he agreed, turning off the lights as I walked down the hallway to the door.

In front of Greater Antioch, off of South Carrollton, Meishelle looked beautiful as she got out of the white Rolls Royce. The caramel colored, brick, steeple church could be seen from a few blocks away. The bell chimed as the three o'clock hour came.

She wore a white, stone decorated, mermaid style gown with no train and her hanging diamond earrings, chocker necklace with surrounding tear drops, and bracelet. She wore a crown with no veil to signify her royalty for the day. She was definitely a Queen.

Our red dresses with the off white and silver flowers were gorgeous. Janasia stepped out of the limo with a grin as bright as the sun. I wanted to knock the smile clean off her face.

Meishelle came over quickly, "No bitch can have power unless you let them."

Hugging her tightly and changing the subject, I said, "You look so stunning, sis."

"So do you, chick. Let me look at you." She held her arm back so she could check me out. "You look beautiful."

"Thanks, boo," I said with enthusiasm.

The photographer took us into the back room of the church. A few photos were taken of us hugging, me handing her the bouquet, and me reseating her crown. I also gave her something old in a box. It was a platinum locket with two pictures we took as teenagers at Walmart.

"You can't cry and ruin your makeup." Her eyes welled with tears. "Are you okay?" She looked into my eyes with concern.

"Yep. Never better." I put on my usual act. "Let's get this started, Mrs. Baptiste."

She remained in the back room to make her grand entrance. The church was decorated with red and off white bows on each pew. In the front stood candles stands that lit the way down the aisle.

Na'Siah looked so handsome in his tux. He nervously stared at all the people in the congregation when the doors opened for him to walk down the aisle.

"Do you see Grandma up there in the front?" I whispered in his ear.

He nodded his head.

"Walk straight to her and smile." I directed him. He followed my directions perfectly.

When the doors opened for my turn, I plastered a smile on my face and focused intensely on maintaining my balance. It was a good thing we weren't doing anything fancy. The tablets were doing their job and the last thing I wanted to do was trip or fall. Quincy made funny faces at me that almost caused me to burst out laughing while Na'Siah waved at me excitedly. I made sure to keep my eyes off of the bridesmaid's section.

Quincy broke down as Meishelle's father gave her hand to him in marriage. I had only seen that twice in my life. The ceremony was short and to the point. Outside of the church, the newlyweds released two white doves.

On our way to the reception, Na'Siah wiggled in his seat. He wanted to come with us instead of riding with the other groomsmen.

"Mommy, you look so pretty. You too, Stone."

"Thanks, baby. But, Stone looks handsome, not pretty."

"What's that?" he asked, Na'Siah sounded confused.

"The man word for *pretty*."

"Okay. Stone, mommy said you look handsome, not pretty."

"Appreciate that man," Stone acknowledged his compliment.

"No problem," he said, causing us to laugh. *These kids today,* I thought.

I felt the effects of my Lithium wearing off, but I didn't take another. Meishelle had already seen through it so I know my momma and Hattie Mae would.

"Take notes because we're next," Stone tried to lighten the mood as we parked to get out.

"And you know this," I put on a smile.

"That's my girl."

The Presidential Palace in Kenner was elegant. Walking through the glass double doors, everyone applauded the couple as the deejay introduced them.

Tables sat alongside each side of the marble floor that sparkled from the overhead chandeliers. Between two columns sat the four tier wedding cake and the Fleur-de-lis grooms cake.

The buffet table and bar were full of people trying to get their eat and drink on. After the pictures, Stone and I shared the bridal party's dance together and then went to the table reserved for the groom's family.

"Hey, Daddy and Mariah," my baby hollered while stuffing his mouth with a sandwich. The usual politeness was shown to Craig and she was invited, but not to sit with the rest of the family. Lately they had been very peaceful, but I seriously doubted it would last much longer.

"Hey, Daddy's man. You enjoying yourself?" Quameer responded.

"Uh huh," Na'Siah mumbled while still trying to eat.

Mariah went over to hug her dad and they started a conversation.

Janasia appeared out of nowhere, standing behind me and Stone, "Hi. How has everyone been?"

Stone immediately grabbed my hand and gripped it tightly. Everyone looked in amazement that she had the audacity to come our way.

Mariah couldn't stand her ass either, "Bitch what is it you want? No one likes you this way."

The same way Janasia snatched Quameer from me, Mariah took him from her, but Janasia didn't go without a fight. She played on Mariah's phone all hours of the night and they eventually had a fight in which Janasia slashed Mariah's face with a razor. The scar looked much better and could be concealed with make-up, but it was permanent. Mariah swore that if she got the chance to fight fair she would whip her ass.

"I just came over to be cordial and extend my deepest sympathies to Krissett. I wanted to tell her how sorry I was to hear her news," Janasia mockingly placed her hand on her heart. All eyes instantly went on me. Stone bore a bewildered face at what she could be referring to. "Oh, you hadn't told them yet about the test you had?" Her question was inquisitive. "Well let me personally extend my sincere apologizes on finding out you're sterile."

How could this bitch have known? I questioned myself. I searched the catalogue of my memory to remember. I recognized her voice now, but had been too distraught that day to pay attention. The nurse that came in after my procedure to ask me if I needed anything was Janasia. That trifling ass bitch must have gone through my fuckin' chart! Her hate must have run deep to put her job on the line. I was definitely reporting her ass.

I dropped my head. Stone searched my face for an answer, but I couldn't bring myself to look at him. My momma and grandmother's shattered eyes revealed the pain they felt for me. Even Mariah looked on in disgust.

Quincy stepped in her face through clenched teeth and said, "Bitch, get your ass out of my reception."

"Quincy doesn't want that now, *do you*?" She shifted her weight in anticipation of his answer. "You want me to tell Meishelle the skeletons in your closet?"

The table's attention shifted from me to him. That thot was on a roll with the foolishness. My legs shook under the table, willing me not to jump up and beat Janasia ass for everything she had done. Her jealously turned to spite when she became pregnant and Quameer forced her into an abortion. I had no part in his decision, but because I had a baby for him, in her mind, I could take the blame. Females could be so vengeful it was ridiculous, but for her to be that old made it pitiful.

"What the fuck are you talking about?" Quincy spat.

"That's funny you acting like you don't know, because you wouldn't have been fucking me to shut me up these past few months if you didn't," she challenged him.

"Man get the fuck out of here with that shit. I wouldn't touch your antique ass.

Meishelle walked behind him and added, "Today, I won't, but the next time I see you I can promise you an ass whooppin' you will never forget. You are so triflin'."

"Trifling with everything functioning. Can't say the same now can you, Krissett?"

They had to give me credit for at least trying. This bitch was the reason I was in this situation. For her to think she would walk away with her life meant she had to be crazy. Grabbing the knife I used to cut up Na'Siah's meat, I jumped up from the table. I would make that dull knife work to eradicate that ho.

Stone snapped out of his daze and tried to restrain me, but not before the knife mad a small cut on her cheek. Guests looked on at the commotion as Janasia eyes bucked and she screamed.

Mariah came around the table as if she was about to walk off, but instead hit her with two across the face. Janasia was caught off guard and hit the floor.

"Catch back is a bitch. I told you I would get your ass," Mariah pounced on her as she kicked wildly, landing blow after blow on her.

Janasia's scalp began to bleed as Mariah pulled human hair braids out by the masses.

Quameer stood by for a minute, watching her get served. Even her family did nothing as they knew her messy ass was getting what she deserved. The owners of the established called the police, who took no time to arrive. Quameer finally stepped in when he heard police sirens outside. It didn't take them long, but Mariah had definitely done a good job on the bitch.

"You too fuckin' disrespectful! I'm sick of your stank ass," Mariah said, spitting on her as a parting gift.

The room parted like the Red Sea as the police came through. Mariah was automatically arrested for her part in the fight.

Helping her bloody ass from the floor, she screamed, "She tried to cut me with a knife!" Janasia pointed like I was in a police lineup.

Oh, shit! With all the damn commotion, I had never put the knife away.

Stone stood on the same side I was holding it, took the knife from my hand and slid it behind his back.

"What the fuck are you talking about?" I held my hands out in front of me. "I didn't do shit to you. You came over here with your bullshit," I blamed her.

"Ma'am, can anyone corroborate your accusation?" The officer turned back around to face Janasia.

I wiggled my fingers and smiled wickedly at her like I had pulled a magician's vanishing act trick.

Janasia's eyes pleaded for someone to agree with her. Meishelle's mother shook her head and spoke up.

"You should be ashamed of yourself, Janasia, ruining this special day."

"Ma'am, there is nothing we can do based on just your word. She has no knife in her hand at this time," the officer explained. "However, since you were involved in the domestic disturbance we responded to you will have to be placed under arrest." He removed his handcuffs.

She turned around and peered at me intently stabbing me with her eyes. I waved bye and smiled. *Got you for now, dumb bitch,* I thought.

Once she and Mariah were removed from the reception, we began to pack up and leave. Loading the last gifts in the car, I gave Meishelle a hug.

"I'm really sorry about this," I embraced her tightly. My heart was just as broken imagining my day. A woman's wedding is one of the happiest moments of her life. To have a portion of it ruined is tragic.

"It's ok. You warned me in a way," she tried to make light of the situation, but the gloom in her eyes revealed the truth.

I closed the door to Quincy's car and waved them off.

Walking over to Stone, I approached him with caution not knowing what to say. I wanted to blame him. *If he had just sat down on the bed, I would have told him myself,* I reasoned.

"We need to talk the minute we get home. I ain't trying to have this conversation up in here." Without another word spoken he turned and walked out the reception hall. We made it as far as the living room of the house before Stone went in with his interrogation.

"Krissett, I don't believe hearsay, so I'm going to ask you myself. Is what that old ho said true?" He raised my chin to look him in the face.

"Yes," I whispered, finally coming clean with my confession.

"After all the shit we been through, you couldn't be real with me, fa real, ma? That's some fucked up shit," his face revealed the wounds of my truth.

"I swear I wanted to Stone. The shit was eating me up inside, but you were so excited about it I didn't know how to kill your hopes and I damn sure don't want to risk losing you." My insides quivered in anxiety on the status of our relationship.

"That's bullshit!" He barked. "How many times I told you that I had you? I'm not playing with you. I put a damn ring on your finger. You did that shit bad, Krissett." He slammed the house door without giving me a chance to respond.

Don't Fu#k With My Heart

Chapter 24

Those were the last words spoken for at least a week unless absolutely necessary. We went and came like two strangers in the night. Nothing I could utter seemed adequate enough to use for the apology I owed him. There was no way to fix the issue of Stone wanting to have a baby with me.

He came home from his overnight job at the end of the week with a small teddy bear. The stomach was embroidered with the words *Always & Forever*. I hadn't been sleeping much so I was up enjoying episodes of Wicked Attraction.

"Good morning," he brushed my nose with my gift, mimicking the kissing sound.

"Good morning. How are you?" I affectionately snuggled with my present.

He sighed and sat down on the bed. "If we are going to do this we can't hold secrets, period. It doesn't matter how we think it will affect each other."

"Stone, how was I supposed to look you in the face? Baby we will never be able to have a seed truly of our own."

"There are other options to have a baby, this shit doesn't define us."

"What other options? I'll miss out on almost everything with the alternatives. You'll never rub or talk to my belly, or hold my hand for ultrasounds. Those are the things I want."

"But Krissett, I will still love you 'til the end of my life. We gon' work through this together."

"You promise?"

"I promise," he said. "Now come put me to sleep."

"I love it when you nasty, Daddy." I pulled out his cone and went to work.

***

Early the next morning I received two dozen pink and red roses with a white teddy bear and a card that read, *More to come, I Love You.* There was no signature.

That evening we became tourists in our own city. Parking by Canal Place we walked the Riverfront, holding hands as the sun set on the banks of the Mississippi. We sat on a bench overlooking Jackson Square, a large fenced square that was decorated with different color flowers, green shrubbery and trees. In the middle sat an iron statue of Andrew Jackson. Outside sat the historic St. Louis Cathedral and the original City Hall, the Cabildo.

"This would be my second choice of a location for our wedding. The white horse drawn carriage would pull up in front of the park. Visitors would stop to see us become husband and wife."

"It's whatever you want, babe. I'm just the husband. Come on," he said, grabbing me by the hand.

"Where are we going?" I asked as we descended the stairs toward Jackson Square.

Across the street sat horse drawn carriages that gave tours of the French Quarter. "Pick one," he instructed me.

"You serious?" My eyes glowed.

"Would I bring you over here if I wasn't?"

"Okay. I like that one," I pointed at the yellow carriage pulled by a big, brown horse.

"Okay. Wait right here as I speak with the gentleman coaching the ride."

Stone returned and hopped on as they pulled the carriage to where he left me standing. Extending his hand he asked, "You coming, babe?"

"Yeah," I accepted and hopped on. I laid my head on his shoulder as we rode around the city for the next thirty minutes. The building lights lit up and added to the romantic ambience. Pointing at different store fronts throughout the Quarters, Stone just smiled back.

Arriving back on Decatur Street in front the Square, Stone helped me down and paid the driver. With his arm around my neck tightly, we walked back to the parking lot by Canal Place for the truck. That night, instead of sex we just held each other.

He and Na'Siah presented me with breakfast in bed over the weekend.

"Stone let me put the cheese in your grits, Mommy," he said, proud of his job.

"And it tastes great with it," I showed my appreciation.

***

Stone had planned a day for me and Na'Siah beginning at the Zoo.

"We need to pick a date for the wedding so we can start saving," he mentioned while Na'Siah ran ahead of us to see the monkeys.

"As far as I am concerned at this point, after Quincy's wedding debacle we can go to the justice of the peace," I replied,' recalling how the reception ended with the police.

We ended up cutting the cake at Quincy and Meishelle's house the following weekend. This time Janasia or Mariah weren't invited to absolutely ensure no drama popped off.

"You sure? Every woman wants a big show. I want whatever you want." Stone checked.

"I'm positive. We can celebrate our one year anniversary with a big wedding," I kissed him on the lips.

"Well, let's start working on the license and do it next month."

"Stop playing, man," I nudged his arm.

"I'm serious. We can invite all your immediate family and mine," he proposed.

"Let's do it." I locked our hands and swung them in the air.

We discussed exploring other alternative options for starting our family. First and foremost Stone wanted me to have a second testing done just to be sure the results were accurate. If it confirmed the initial findings we could check into the surgical option of having my tubes unblocked if possible. The last resort would be a surrogate or adoption. I shot down the surrogate idea the minute it left his lips. After this threesome, no woman was taking part in our equation.

He asked if we still had the threesome planned. I told him I would check with Cionna about when she would be coming back. I was down as long as he kept to my expectations. On the inside I was more than okay with it, a change which had me feeling some type of way. Since she'd left, Cionna had been in my dreams a couple of times. There was one dream where the action between us caused me to wake up with a drenched pussy. I thought maybe Stone's mouth had explored me over night after hearing my moans while sleeping. I knew better though, I wouldn't have been able to sleep through that.

"I think you say certain things for me to assure you that you're the only woman I want."

"Maybe so," I replied slyly and laughed. "I can never grow tired of the man that has my heart telling me the feeling is mutual."

He raised my hand up and kissed it "You're my everything, ma."

"Ditto, boo."

Chapter 25

The first three days of the following week I received more flower arrangements, accompanied by a separate gift of chocolates, gift certificates, and balloons. Monday the card read, *Our Future*. Tuesday, *More and More Each Day*. Wednesday, *Nothing Without You*. My office began to look like I majored in horticulture.

Each morning Stone came home from work, I showed my gratitude for the gifts by putting something on him to help his ass to sleep. I appreciated him on the kitchen table, in the Jacuzzi, and in the garage.

I hit up Cionna by text to check on her and arrange the threesome. She told me her mother was doing better and she should be home within the next week. Stone and I agreed to get married in a month and half. We had already applied for the marriage license. I asked if it could be the week after she came home, I wanted to avoid inviting another woman into my bed after my last name changed to Robertson. It was strictly me and him against the world. She said it would be a push but she would let me know.

The next Sunday evening he asked me to meet him at Hurwitz Mintz on Airline Highway with Na'Siah. The elongated, two story, pink showroom held some of the most expensive furniture. We had talked about getting new furniture during the week, but I didn't see a need. Our house was nicely furnished already, besides, at that store the bed alone could probably go for three thousand.

Stone was waiting in the lobby. A middle aged black lady greeted us, "Hi my name is Susan. Is there anything I can help you with?"

"Yes, we are interested in furniture for our new home. I'd like to start out with a bedroom and living room set."

"I'll be glad to show you what we have. The living rooms are right this way," she directed us to the left side of the showroom.

"What new house?" I grabbed his arm to keep him from proceeding.

"The one we're going to look at next week."

"Huh?" I thought my ears were playing tricks on me.

"With our expanded unit we will need more space. Na'Siah doesn't want to have to share a room with his brother or sister, do you?" He asked as he looked to my son.

"No," Na'Siah shook his head defiantly.

"We have the guest bedroom that can be converted into a nursery," I recommended.

"Not an option. I want to keep that room for company. Now let's look around, please," he ushered me toward the living room sets.

Me and Meishelle hooked up for lunch the next day at Twin Peaks, a restaurant along the lines of Hooters. I was personally telling each of my ladies of the change in plans regarding the big wedding. I expected Meishelle to be easy like Schtanya and Hattie Mae were. My momma was livid that she would have to wait a year for the big shindig. Quincy, I called on the phone. He shared his usual negative thoughts, but asked for the location details and time when he realized he wasn't changing my mind.

"Hey, married lady," I embraced her as she walked in. "How is married life treating you?"

"Hey, chick, I missed you," she returned the sentiment. "It's treating me okay."

"Okay? Girl, please, no one can contact y'all after sunset."

"Me and my man need to relax each other after work," she laughed.

"Yuck! *TMI*," I covered my mouth.

In addition to my nuptials was my upcoming court date for Janasia who had made a full recovery. Meishelle said her eye was black, she had a hickey and was missing patches of hair throughout her head. The low down bitch pressed charges against me for aggravated assault since I was the one who pulled the knife on her. I found a decent criminal lawyer to handle the charges, he was sure I would only get probation.

My custody attorney was concerned that the judge would consider my behavior in the matter and count it against me. I truly hoped that wasn't the case.

I changed the subject back to the wedding and as expected it went very smoothly. We set up a date for the upcoming weekend to look for a nice dress. My preference was a simple, satin fabric, off white, floor length gown. I looked forward to the time with my girl again. We were back where we'd left off.

Don't Fu#k With My Heart

Chapter 26

The stunning rays of sunlight from the window congratulated me on the morning of my wedding. The license had been issued and my day had finally arrived. I was ecstatic.

"Guess what day it is?" My momma came from the adjoining room with a silver platter.

I had rented individual suites for me, Hattie Mae, my momma, Meishelle, and Schtanya. My house was all in boxes as we prepared for our move. We would be moving within the next few weeks into the five bedroom house in Lakeview we had closed on.

"For me?" I slid up in the bed, propping the pillows behind my back.

She placed the tray on my lap and lifted up the top. I gasped and covered my mouth. Next to the breakfast plate was a pair of diamond earrings, bracelets, and a necklace.

"I had to get my baby her something new." She placed the necklace around my neck and kissed my cheek. I moved the tray and enthusiastically jumped out of the bed like a little girl.

"Thank you, Momma," I squeezed her securely.

"How you feeling today?"

"Indescribable." It was the first word that came to mind, but there was really no one word to capture my sentiments.

She ushered me back to the bed to eat breakfast but I never finished. Hattie Mae came to present me with my something old.

"For my baby girl." She handed me with a box that contained an exquisite pearl hair pen. "This goes all the way back to your great, great grandmother. I'm hoping you will wear your hair up today. You make me so proud." Tears streamed down her face at the same time they cascaded down mine.

"I love you so much." I reached out for her hand and held it tightly.

Meishelle gave me a small gift bag when it was her turn. "This is the day I have dreamed of for you. I pray a million more come your way."

Schtanya went next. "There's no way to express the happiness I have in being a part of your special day." She gave me an extra gift which was a fourteen karat gold watch to be worn on special occasions.

"I don't know what to say to all of you," I was so choked up I struggled to gain control of my speech. I embraced each one of them.

"We will leave you alone for a few minutes to gather your thoughts and then come back to help you dress," Hattie Mae ushered everyone out the door. I sat and reflected on my past.

The lies, deceptions, and betrayals that all led me to this moment. They all played a key role in helping me to fulfill my destiny of finding a good man. One who loved, appreciated, and cherished me through every fault. I wanted to scream from the tallest skyscraper to let everyone know that I had made it. I had found my one true love, my prince charming.

My phone vibrated on the nightstand.

7:55 a.m.: Can't wait for you to be my wife. See you shortly.

7:56 a.m.: Can't wait to take you as my husband. Xoxo

My girl Mika knocked on the door about thirty minutes later to do my hair and makeup. She did soft curls that she pinned up using the hair pen Hattie Mae had given me.

Glancing in the mirror, I took a deep breath. My eyes sparkled in the reflection, verifying that I was an astonishing woman inside and out.

Everyone came back into the room for the photographer. He took a few pictures of some slight touch ups to my hair and makeup. Everyone took turns zipping my dress, a little at a time until it was at my neck. This was a once in a lifetime moment that I would never get back.

I spun around on my heels, doing my final check in the mirror.

"You ready, Ms. Baptiste?" Meishelle asked.

"Been ready all my life." I picked up my bouquet and followed behind them.

Our appointment was for eleven that morning. Quincy, Stone, and his family awaited our arrival. His grandmother had her usual sour face, but she couldn't steal my joy on this glorious day.

He kissed me on the lips when I reached him. "You ready to become Mrs. Robertson?" he inquired.

"With everything in me."

Craig took my arm and walked me into the chambers. I tried to hold back the tears so my makeup wouldn't run. The Judge read the traditional vows and we each said I do, presenting each other with rings. Meishelle and Quincy stepped forward to sign their signatures as witnesses, although we had so many more.

"I now pronounce you man and wife. You may kiss your bride." The passionate meeting of our lips was breathtaking.

Stone's mother and sister showered me with hugs while his grandmother stood to the side. When the photographer took pictures of the family, she declined to be in any of them. I had no clue why she even bothered to come, but Stone addressed it.

"Like it or not grams this is my wife now. You need to respect that," Stone voice told his seriousness.

"I don't have to do a damn thing. I'm grown," she spat.

"Krissett hasn't done anything to you. Why would you come to act ugly?" Her words seemed to have hurt him.

"She changed you and I don't like who you have become. I came believing that you would have enough sense not to marry her ass."

Not today, Krissett, I told myself. I was thrilled that my momma and everyone else had gone to get the car. My family would have flown off the hinges on her.

"No one can change me. I changed for myself and she helped me. You should be proud of who I have become," Stone rebutted.

She issued no response, instead she walked off.

"It's ok, baby." I attempted to reassure him, but I knew he was hurting. I never had ill feelings for the elderly, but she was pushing me.

Stone hung his head in disappointment, "Come on, babe."

We went to eat at Ruth Chris' with everyone who attended. Stone's grandmother made his mother bring her home first. He feigned smiles, but it was obvious he was anything but happy. I was really feeling some type of way toward his grandmother because I believed she purposely showed up to ruin our day. There was a demon in that woman.

After lunch we went back to the room. We had postponed the official honeymoon until after we got settled into the new house. Cionna wasn't able to do the threesome before the wedding, so I would surprise him with it when we returned. Her mother's radiation treatments were causing other complications and she could do little for herself. I encouraged her to take care of her business, me and Stone weren't going anywhere. I deep massaged his shoulders to remove some of the tension he had and he later reciprocated. Our kisses turned into extraordinary back to back love making sessions, but this time they felt different. Stone was no longer just my boyfriend, he was now my husband.

Don't Fu#k With My Heart

Chapter 27

We were lying in bed watching a movie for the night when Stone's phone vibrated. Checking his ID, his face twisted in aggravation.

"Yeah," he answered. After a full minute of silence, he remarked with agitation in his tone, "Are you serious?" I sat up in the bed.

"What's wrong?" I mouthed as I unwrapped my arms from around him.

"Alright then," he scoffed before hanging up and releasing a deep sigh. "Urgh! Dude didn't show up for his shift and they want me to come in." Creases of frustration wrinkled his forehead.

"Babe, it's okay," I said gently. Although I didn't want him to remove his body from next to mine, the money would come in handy for either the house or spending money on our vacation.

"You going to come with me?" he offered.

"Nah. I'll have Mr. Teddy to keep me company." I grabbed the bear he bought for me off the nightstand.

"Ok." Stone rose out of bed and begrudgingly pulled on his work clothes. When he was dressed, he leaned done and gave me a kiss. "You absolutely sure you don't want to come and keep me company?" he confirmed.

"No, boo. I don't feel like getting up."

"Call me if you change your mind. It would my first opportunity to beat my wife's pussy up in the office."

"Next time, baby," I promised.

"I'm going to hold you to it, Krissett."

"Please do," I cooed.

After Stone left, I couldn't seem to go to sleep. For three hours I tossed and turned in the bed. I had grown used to him being at home with me during the night for the last week. Sensing that sleep would never come, I remained in my lingerie, got my bag together and headed out the door. I decided against calling Stone so it would be a surprise when I arrived. If he wanted wanted to beat this kitty up in his office, that's exactly what I was going to let him do.

As I drove toward his job, I had to squeeze my legs together to contain the purring that had already began to mount. I imagined him bending me over a desk and making me scream his name. I turned off my headlights as I pulled through the gate. He usually left the office door open and I was hoping he had done so again so that I wouldn't have to knock. I was going to walk right in there, disrobe without saying a word, and make this night memorable. I grabbed my bag and sashayed across the parking lot in my stiletto heels, they made me look so much sexier.

Nearing the building, I could hear the unit on the side running and the windows were fogged up. Stopping to peak through them, I could scarcely make out the light from the TV surveillance monitors. Feeling naughty, I tiptoed the last few steps, slowly turning the knob in case he was in the office instead of making the rounds. I hoped the door wouldn't creek and announce my presence before he was able to behold my outfit.

As soon as I stepped inside, my mouth and my heart hit the floor! Stone was leaned back in a chair with his legs spread out. His eyes were closed and his head was thrown back in utter ecstasy because some bitch was down on her knees sucking his dick! His hands gripped the back of her head tightly and he guided her head up and down his shaft.

"Umm," he moaned.

"*Motherfucker!*" I dropped my bag in the doorway and charged straight toward him.

He pushed the ho down and jumped up trying to fix his pants.

"Baby, it's not what it looks like."

"What the fuck you mean?" I railed as my hand shot up and connected with his face. *Whap!* "So, nigga, you didn't just have your dick in that bitch's mouth!" *Bam*! I punched him dead in his lying face.

As Stone staggered back, I looked down at the ho who was just rising to her feet. She looked up with a smirk on her face and wiped her mouth. "I told you he would be back," Takeisha spewed vengefully.

"Bitch, you're about to die!" I snarled.

Before she could get to her feet I took the huge binder full of paper and swung it with all my strength. *Bam*! Her face twisted to the left and blood spewed from her mouth. I pounced on her, hitting her with a quick right and left jab. As I straddled Takeisha's body and commenced to pummeling her trifling ass, the pain of Stone's betrayal rose up in my chest and my fists fell to my sides. I blinked back the tears that threatened to fall. *Not this time*, I thought.

Nothing about him had changed. Quincy was absolutely right, Stone had simply talked some fire jail house talk. He sold me promises of a future, of happiness, instead he served me the same fate as Quameer and Hollow. Spending time with my son, parading him around and acting like he cared. I even considered eating another bitch pussy to please his ass. There was nothing I wouldn't do for that man.

I was the one who ran back and forth to prison on his visitation days, struggled to maintain a house, his books, and a jail account to talk to him. No one else. His own family wouldn't give me a fucking dime for him. Hell, I paid for the majority of the fucking coming home party with my student loan money. The clothes to rebuild his wardrobe? I paid that. Maybe he had a stash, but that money was hidden from me.

I carried the weight of the house, allowing him to feel more like a man. He was paying bills with *my* hard earned money. His jobs didn't pay shit, so I had probably paid for my engagement and wedding ring. The flowers, gifts, closing costs on that new fucking house. Furniture and moving expenses. If he had only given me a tithe of ten percent, that would have been a lot. I beat myself up for not being able to give him the family he wanted, but I would've only been further fucking myself by having a child with him.

Fuck that! There was nothing wrong with me, I had been the decent one. Quameer, Mariah, Janasia, Hollow, and other faces of those that hurt me in the past surrounded me in a circle, laughing and taunting me for being so stupid and thinking that Stone was any different than them.

I scrambled to my feet and in my fury I reached out and violently swept everything off of the desk. Tools clanged on the bare floor and intensified the drumming in my head.

Stone was just standing there looking stupid. My eyes were furnaces. "You petty motherfucker!" I spat as I visually searched for an object to bash his goddamn head in with.

Lo and behold, a hammer laid right at my feet. I reached down and snatched it up and held it like a billy club. Then I stepped toward Stone, intent on leaving his skull shattered in tiny pieces. "You were supposed to be different!" I swung the hammer, smashing one of the surveillance monitors. My heart pummeled in my chest, each beat shooting an agonizing pain through my entire body.

Stone stepped forward and tried to wrap his arms around me. His voice was lowered to a gentle tone but that nigga still sounded like Judas. "Krissett, baby, calm down and let me explain," he attempted.

"Get the fuck off of me!" I raised the hammer at him and he backed up. "Why am I just not enough for you?" Tears clouded my vision as I continued with my demolition of the small office. The harder I cried, the more destruction I caused. My words became inaudible as I clobbered one computer after another.

Whatever Stone and that bitch Takeisha was doing while I wreaked havoc, I was oblivious to it because I was in a blind rage. Through the fog of my heartache and anger I heard Stone plead, "Baby, please calm down. This shit don't make no sense."

I stopped and whirled around in his direction. "What? *It don't make no sense?*" I repeated his dumb ass response. "You black ass bastard! I trusted you with my heart after this bitch warned me about you!" I threw the hammer through the window causing shards of glass to take spray all over the room. My heart shattered along with it. "How could you do this shit to me?" I wailed.

Stone grabbed me in a bear hug. "Krissett—"

"Nigga, let go of me!"

"Calm down and I will. Baby, remember—"

"No, you remember, motherfucker!" I screamed, cutting him off. "Remember our vows, 'til death do us part. Well, it's about to part us tonight!"

"Babe, it wasn't what you think. I love you, Krissett," he offered lamely.

"No the fuck you don't. You looked me in the eye when you came home from prison and promised me that you were a different man. I am your *wife!*" My body draped over his arm like a towel from the stinging in my chest. "You vowed to cherish me." My legs became crippled, giving out. He tightened his grip, holding me up. My nostrils flared seeing Takeisha rushing around the room to get her clothes, "Let me go," I fumed. Her pants lay close to my feet. She looked at me, contemplating whether she should leave without them or not. The stupid bitch decided to try me and I landed a kick right to her face. Blood gushed from her nose.

"You trifling trick! Who's the bad bitch now?" I found spit from within my soul and hocked it at her.

Stone lifted his arm a little higher to restrain me more. I bit into his arm and lock jawed like a pit bull onto it, refusing to let go until he released me from his grip. His skin tore, revealing flesh and he could no longer hold onto me.

"Fuck, Krissett!" He hollered as I rushed over to get in my duffle bag.

Knowing that I kept the gun there, Stone reached out and grabbed me with his other arm. He barely missed and I fell to the floor in the process of ducking him. He attempted to grab my foot, but I kicked at him squarely in his face. About an inch more, my heel would have penetrated his eye ball.

"What the fuck is wrong with you?" He held his face.

Scurrying to the bag on my hands and knees, I blindly felt through the items until I felt the clip on the Nine I carried everywhere with me. It was fully loaded. All I needed to do was take the safety off. These muthafuckas were dead because there was no way out as I was blocking the only door.

Stone silently raised his hands in surrender while Takeisha's bloodcurdling screams could probably be heard for miles. I aimlessly fired off two shots, one shattering another window and the other lodged in the sofa less than ten feet from her head.

Stone lunged at me, pinning me to the ground, wrestling me for the gun. The gun slid across the floor.

"Hear me out," he demanded.

"I didn't wrong you! Why would you want to do this to me?" My tears ran down into my ears. "I can't keep going through this anymore," I reiterated over and over, my body jerked from my inflamed nerves.

"Takiesha, get the fuck out of here. Run! Now!" he growled.

"You taking up for this bitch!" I shrieked as I struggled to get from under his weight to the gun.

"Baby, look at me," he pushed my face in his direction, but I shook it back and forth rebelliously.

"You were supposed to be my happily ever after, Stone. How could you?" Horrific pins and needles of anguish pierced my spirit.

Takeisha tried to dash past me, but I slashed her ankle with a shard of glass that I had inched toward. "Ugh!" She squealed, falling to the floor grabbing her ankle.

"I will kill you, bitch," I promised sadistically. The fear in her eyes showed as the puddle of blood began to cover the floor. Seeing her blood on my hands sent a chilling sensation of satisfaction my down spine, and I thirsted for more.

She grabbed her ankle, sliding across the floor to the wall, scaling it to get out of the office. The trail of blood left behind revealed her wound was serious. I used the glass to try and stab Stone until I finally impaled the center of his hand.

"Motherfucker!" he winced. "Krissett, look at me, ma." I wiggled from under him and scrambled to my feet with him on my heels. Reaching the gun, Stone tried to subdue me again, but was limited because of his hand. It was bleeding profusely.

"I warned you not to fuck with my heart, Stone." My chest filled with pure rage. The tears had stopped flowing, and I saw him clear enough to fire a direct shot to his heart.

Stone was bleeding profusely, but he still had enough strength to put up a fight, though.

"You don't want to do this. This isn't you," he petitioned as the struggle for my gun ensued.

I conquered enough of the gun to get to the trigger, but Stone wriggled with the clip, trying to free it from the gun. We battled, knocking against the chair and sofa. I wasn't giving up until he was dead.

"Boom! Boom!"

It sounded off as we both fell. Blood seeped onto the floor from the wound. I felt emotionless and void as I watched it spread across the floor, my skin feeling cold and wet...

To Be Continued...

Don't Fu#k With My Heart II

Available Now!

Stay Connected with Us!

Text **LOCKDOWN** to 22828 to stay up-to-date with new releases, sneak peaks, contests and more…

Thank you!

Submission Guideline.

Submit the first three chapters of your completed manuscript to <u>ldpsubmissions@gmail.com</u>, subject line: Your book's title. The manuscript must be in a .doc file and sent as an attachment. Document should be in Times New Roman, double spaced and in size 12 font. Also, provide your synopsis and full contact information. If sending multiple submissions, they must each be in a separate email.

Have a story but no way to send it electronically? You can still submit to LDP/Ca$h Presents. Send in the first three chapters, written or typed, of your completed manuscript to:

LDP: Submissions Dept
Po Box 870494
Mesquite, Tx 75187

DO NOT send original manuscript. Must be a duplicate.

Provide your synopsis and a cover letter containing your full contact information.

Thanks for considering LDP and Ca$h Presents.

Don't Fu#k With My Heart

BOW DOWN TO MY GANGSTA

By **Ca$h**

TORN BETWEEN TWO

By **Coffee**

BLOOD STAINS OF A SHOTTA **III**

By **Jamaica**

WHEN THE STREETS CLAP BACK **II**

By **Jibril Williams**

STEADY MOBBIN

By **Marcellus Allen**

BLOOD OF A BOSS **V**

By **Askari**

BRIDE OF A HUSTLA **III**

By **Destiny Skai**

WHEN A GOOD GIRL GOES BAD **II**

By **Adrienne**

THE HEART OF A GANGSTA **III**

By **Jerry Jackson**

LOYAL TO THE GAME **IV**

By **T.J. & Jelissa**

A DOPEBOY'S PRAYER **II**

By **Eddie "Wolf" Lee**

IF LOVING YOU IS WRONG... **III**

Don't Fu#k With My Heart

LOVE ME EVEN WHEN IT HURTS

By **Jelissa**

DAUGHTERS SAVAGE

By **Chris Green**

BLOODY COMMAS **III**

SKI MASK CARTEL II

By **T.J. Edwards**

TRAPHOUSE KING

By **Hood Rich**

BLAST FOR ME **II**

RAISED AS A GOON V

BRED BY THE SLUMS

By **Ghost**

A DISTINGUISHED THUG STOLE MY HEART **III**

By **Meesha**

ADDICTIED TO THE DRAMA **II**

By **Jamila Mathis**

LIPSTICK KILLAH II

By **Mimi**

THE BOSSMAN'S DAUGHTERS 4

WHAT BAD BITCHES DO

By **Aryanna**

Available Now

RESTRAINING ORDER **I & II**

Don't Fu#k With My Heart

By **CA$H & Coffee**

LOVE KNOWS NO BOUNDARIES **I II & III**

By **Coffee**

RAISED AS A GOON I, II, III & IV

By **Ghost**

LAY IT DOWN **I & II**

LAST OF A DYING BREED

BLOOD STAINS OF A SHOTTA I & II

By **Jamaica**

LOYAL TO THE GAME

LOYAL TO THE GAME II

LOYAL TO THE GAME III

By **TJ & Jelissa**

BLOODY COMMAS I & II

SKI MASK CARTEL

By **T.J. Edwards**

IF LOVING HIM IS WRONG...I & II

By **Jelissa**

WHEN THE STREETS CLAP BACK

By **Jibril Williams**

A DISTINGUISHED THUG STOLE MY HEART I & II

By **Meesha**

PUSH IT TO THE LIMIT

By **Bre' Hayes**

BLOOD OF A BOSS **I, II, III & IV**

Don't Fu#k With My Heart

By **Askari**

THE STREETS BLEED MURDER **I, II & III**

THE HEART OF A GANGSTA I & II

By **Jerry Jackson**

CUM FOR ME

CUM FOR ME 2

CUM FOR ME 3

An **LDP Erotica Collaboration**

BRIDE OF A HUSTLA **I & II**

THE FETTI GIRLS **I, II& III**

By **Destiny Skai**

WHEN A GOOD GIRL GOES BAD

By **Adrienne**

A GANGSTER'S REVENGE **I II III & IV**

THE BOSS MAN'S DAUGHTERS

THE BOSS MAN'S DAUGHTERS II

THE BOSSMAN'S DAUGHTERS III

A SAVAGE LOVE **I & II**

BAE BELONGS TO ME

A HUSTLER'S DECEIT I, II

By **Aryanna**

A KINGPIN'S AMBITON

A KINGPIN'S AMBITION **II**

I MURDER FOR THE DOUGH

By **Ambitious**

Don't Fu#k With My Heart

Don't Fu#k With My Heart

BROOKLYN HUSTLAZ

By **Boogsy Morina**

BROOKLYN ON LOCK I & II

By **Sonovia**

GANGSTA CITY

By **Teddy Duke**

A DRUG KING AND HIS DIAMOND

A DOPEMAN'S RICHES

By Nicole Goosby

BOOKS BY LDP'S CEO, CA$H

TRUST IN NO MAN

TRUST IN NO MAN 2

TRUST IN NO MAN 3

BONDED BY BLOOD

SHORTY GOT A THUG

THUGS CRY

THUGS CRY 2

THUGS CRY 3

TRUST NO BITCH

TRUST NO BITCH 2

TRUST NO BITCH 3

TIL MY CASKET DROPS

RESTRAINING ORDER

RESTRAINING ORDER 2

IN LOVE WITH A CONVICT

Coming Soon

BONDED BY BLOOD 2

BOW DOWN TO MY GANGSTA

Don't Fu#k With My Heart

www.ingramcontent.com/pod-product-compliance
Lightning Source LLC
Chambersburg PA
CBHW070004260626
47159CB00005B/1665